EAGLE'S FLIGHT

in the

AMERICAN REVOLUTION

by

Kim Kacoroski

This book is a work of fiction. Names, characters, places, and incidents are either the product of the author's imagination or are used fictitiously. Any resemblance to actual persons, living or dead, or to actual events or locales is entirely coincidental.

EAGLE'S FLIGHT IN THE AMERICAN REVOLUTION

Copyright © 2013 Kim Kacoroski. All rights reserved, including the right to reproduce this book, or portions thereof, in any form. No part of this text may be reproduced, transmitted, downloaded, decompiled, reverse engineered, or stored in or introduced into any information storage and retrieval system, in any form or by means, whether electronic or mechanical without the express written consent of the author. The scanning, uploading, and distribution of this book via the Internet or via any other means without the permission of the publisher is illegal and punishable by law. Please purchase only authorized electronic editions and do not participate in or encourage electronic piracy of copyrighted materials.

The publisher does not have control over and does not assume any responsibility for the author or third-party websites or their content.

Cover art illustrations by Kim Kacoroski, Phillipe Velasquez, and Masha Tatarintsev

Copyright © 2278133/leonardophoto/iStockphoto

Copyright © 26215702/sekarb/iStockphoto

2nd Edition 2019.6.02

Visit the author website:

https://www.kimkacoroski.com
ISBN: 978-1-947036-28-4 (Paperback)

Book Two of Flight Series

Eagles's Flight in the American Revolution II

Other Books in Flight Series

Flight from Oblivion I

Flight of the Ascendants in the American Revolution III

Choices from the American Revolution IV

Bridges of Flight before the American Revolution V

Testimony VI

Books in the Camelon Series

The Promise of Camelon I

The Dragons of Camelon II

History of the World According to the Druids III

The Kingdom of the Golden Tara V

Bridges of Flight before the American Revolution VI

Books in the Oblivion Series

Escape from Oblivion I

Beyond Oblivion II

Oblivion's Edge III

Oblivion's Deal IV

Flight from Oblivion V

Dedicated to Judith Poole Reed, legal secretary, mother,

and wife (b. 1943 - 2014)

INTRODUCTION

This version of EAGLE'S FLIGHT IN THE AMERICAN REVOLUTION references the tunes used in the original manuscript. Many of the songs came from the pop hits during 1976, the year of the Bicentennial celebration. The melodies provide a two-hundred-old perspective of the American Revolution, which resonate with those willing to listen. Sounds reach into the recesses of the psyche and must be filtered through the lens of the heart. Unlike the eye, which can be closed, ears remain open. Hearing loss serves the agenda of those harboring rigidity and resistance, unless the individual is born deaf. Children often develop ear infections before learning to react to what they don't want to hear. In contrast, a soothing series of notes can stretch the capacity to understand the undercurrents of a given situation. The tune references in the following chapters provide a springboard for the reader to simply dive into the material seasoned over two hundred years.

Chapter One

When the dew of the morning

Rose to meet my lips

I trembled as I drunk in your nakedness

I felt the clarity of discontinued thought

Race with silver mercurial drops down my spine

Towards the mysterious passage called eternity

Without any rhyme of Reason

And void of the shape of things to come

I plunged into the abyss

Hoping to pierce the hollow between us

The unRational became my friend

Having progressed from the shadow of Rationality

Standing forlorn on the edge

I'd know in a heartbeat

In a flicker of an eye

Forever engrained upon my memory

Through the dance of the illusion

Of what we call life

DEWDROPS

Kim Kacoroski © 4/25/1997

"THIS METAPHORICAL FLIGHT into the American Revolution is for you, Dr. Tobias Jones," Dr. Jim Mansfield said, handing a brown-colored ornament to the naturopathic physician sitting on the steps of the front door to his house.

Tobias looked down at the three-inch diameter amulet, which had once been someone's necklace. The metal contained a bronze alloy, and a crystal known as a king's stone adorned the center. He recognized the crystal, which ancients used for astral projection. The pendant resembled the shape of a heart and pieces of coral studded the metal.

"I dreamed about this necklace," Tobias realized. "Where did you get it?"

"An antique store in New Brunswick, Canada," Dr. Mansfield replied. "More than one intuitive said that it belonged to a woman who died in the Battle of Lexington-Concord."

"Someone in the clinic told me that I would be receiving an ornament from the American Revolution," Tobias added. "There is a story in the crystal."

"Yes, the clerk at the store told me that someone had been saving it for you. It came from an estate that liquidated a few months ago. Apparently, she knew the collector well," Dr. Mansfield continued. "What do we have between us? At least eight intuitives saw the crystal before I found it. It goes to you, but it is not a light gift. Your mission is to use it in determining the story, and use it for healing purposes. I want to hear about it. I'm curious. This nation needs to heal, Tobias. The appearance of such a device as this necklace means that the information is critical. Not only that, but we can't trust any information written after 1775 about the United States."

"What do we know so far?" Tobias asked. Without waiting for Dr. Mansfield's response, Tobias answered his own question. "The bearer was a seventeen year old female who died fighting at Lexington-Concord. I bet that she fired the first shot. Remember, they call it the shot that was heard around the world. But, why did she fire the gun? Why did the world hear her shot above the others? They tell me that she had three lovers, and had been a caregiver during the yellow fever epidemic. The chills and cold sweats are embedded in this object. She would have died wearing it. The British soldiers picked it off her body and traded it in their northern outposts, which is why it appeared in Canada. Maine remained a British outpost until shortly before the Civil War."

"My information is that the object represented a family heirloom, passed through five generations of males," Dr. Mansfield said. "They bequeathed to this young woman who died with it. What does that tell you about the direness of the family lineage and struggles? The characters carved on it are from the Hindu language. It is something that a knight would have worn. Temple knights from the occult underground operating Solomon's Temple served as pushers on the Silk Road. I suspect that she worked with Brahmins, like so many of the underestimated colonists. They were knights from Camelon. The device bears testament to their spirituality, something that the history books missed about the American Revolution."

"As usual, to heal the wound, we must rewrite history until the truth comes out," Tobias observed, almost mesmerized by the light refracted between the various surfaces of the multi-layered crystal. "For an object such as this to make its way to me, it must mean that the truth died with this young revolutionary. Being female, fundamental concepts about the parentage of this country are destroyed. We have a founding mother who has come back from the past to reveal her story."

"Yes, Dr. Jones," Dr. Mansfield addressed Tobias. "History is written by the survivors, not necessarily the ones who made it. Throw out the history texts and all other commercial bits of armchair historians. This is not United Fruit of America. It is called the United States of America. The spirituality inherent in the crystal's appearance and inscriptions on the metal tell us that the nation has a more noble foundation than the commerce we have heard so much about."

"It is not the covert maneuverings of a banana-crazed mob," Tobias resounded. "It is more than the fables of 'no taxation without representation.' The foundation of this country was not about the tea or opium dumped in Boston Harbor. It goes far deeper. The issues of the American Revolution were concerned with spiritual survival rather than commerce. In fact, by the appearance of this ornament, it appears that the argument of the colonists was with India rather than the British monarchy."

"Tobias, it goes back to the spice route determined by Marco Polo," Dr. Mansfield told him.

"Yes, Jim, I think that you are correct," Tobias said, weighing the ornament in his hand. "The Eagles fought the American Revolution for transcendence. The desperate deaths of its fighters indicate that is where they found their freedom. It is a sobering thought. This means that the spiritual transcendence can't be copyrighted."

"I agree," Jim said. "The cover-up began with the writers of the Declaration of Independence. Our task is to figure out the unspoken version."

"The words of the assassinated presidents only tried to comfort a dying country. We talked about this earlier," Tobias mentioned. "Nobody listened, which is why this task has presented itself at this late date."

"Like the caregiver of the yellow fever epidemic in Philadelphia, you are the healer on the project. Only this time, the country is the patient," Jim observed. "The bigger question is whether this patient can recover."

"You are correct, Jim," Tobias agreed. "We see it in the eyes of the pathology that comes through the doors of our clinics."

"Great. Tobias, I want a remedy for this patient," Jim directed. "I know you can do it."

"Thanks, Jim, but first the truth must come out. The wound must be healed at its deepest level. Surgeons know this and call this process of healing 'primary intention,'" Tobias acknowledged.

"I know," Jim concurred. He sighed. "Tobias, look into that crystal, and find that teenage female revolutionary. As a colleague, I need to know the story as much as you."

"No, Jim, we are both wrong," Tobias firmly concluded. "The patient is dead. The spirit of the nation went with the wearer of this amulet. We've been in denial. All that is left is this bronze piece, which sounds like a heavy tin can and a king's stone."

"Well, there's the battleground where she fell," Jim reminded, agreeing with Tobias with misty eyes. "The site of the old Green Dragon tavern is somewhere in the back streets of Boston, not far from its new location. Then there is the beer at the City Tavern in Philly, where they all went to party after legislative sessions."

"I don't know how much our young woman would have partied with that crowd," Tobias reflected as he cocked his head from side to side. At the moment, he could not determine an answer from the object in his hands. He looked at Jim for insight.

"I suspect that she occasionally enjoyed a good beer, perhaps some chowder or shepherd's pie," Jim reassured Tobias. "Something on the light side. She had a war to fight and obviously kept a watchful eye on the legal beagles."

"You're right," Tobias speculated. "She would have needed to keep up her strength to wear such a heavy ornament. I can imagine her walking with uneven shoulders from years of shouldering a musket with a kickback."

"Yes, I visualize that also," Jim remarked. "They didn't design ergonomic his and her muskets. She seemed the type of individual who would have practiced her shot until her gun literally became her arm."

"I think we have our woman," Tobias observed. "Thanks for the piece of history, Jim. I want to run this information by a friend who is an osteopath. Let's have lunch next Friday, maybe I'll have more to report by then."

"Wonderful!" Jim exclaimed. "Keep me in the loop. After retrieving this necklace as a point of reference, I'll believe almost anything."

Tobias nodded and laughed. He waved at Jim before he dashed inside his car. Gazing at the woods surrounding his property, he turned around and headed for the steps of his front porch. After entering his home, he went straight to his home office and placed the necklace on his desk so that it faced him. He punched the buttons on his phone for Dr. Joan Standish, DO. Making the most of the three hour time difference between them, he suspected that he could reach her at home by now.

"Hi, Tobias," she answered as she identified the caller on the machine.

Studying the reflections and light within the layers of the king's stone, Tobias related his story concerning the necklace. A few seconds of silence ensued while he waited for Joan's observations.

"It's an Eagle's Flight," she commented. "Nothing remains except the imprint on the supraconsciousness. This is where the real story begins."

"Eagles soar high into the heavens compared to the other birds," Tobias rejoined. "They connote spiritual heights, particularly with respect to the more grounded turkey."

"Some contend that Franklin proposed the turkey for a national symbol," Joan said.

"Yeah, but I suspect that Franklin argued just to get people to think. He had a rhetorical side," Tobias acknowledged. "He often assumed positions that he knew were unpopular, but penetrating. He could not be discounted."

"We are dealing with a bird with a very refined nervous system, exhibiting great control under stressful conditions. A turkey would die from shock from a flying drop and roll maneuver used to catch small prey at distances. Unlike the buzzard or hawk, the eagle sports characteristic grace and winged elegance. Hawks are more compact, and hunt intensely. The body of the eagle was designed to fly high, and yet miss nothing below. The eagle's eyes detect the smallest motion on the ground."

"Great," Tobias started. "The American Revolution viewed from this vantage point, an overview that picks out the life in the dead terrain. Got it."

"One other thing," Joan interjected. "It is all about personal relationships."

"Where did you get that notion?" Tobias quizzed her.

"I don't know," she replied. "I sense that it has something to do with the necklace. Loners didn't exist in the American Revolution. The war constituted either interdependency or codependency."

"Not bad for a group claiming independence," Tobias remarked.

"Now we just have to figure out exactly what that means," Joan speculated. "Then there is the question of the flag. Allegiance at this point remained out of the question."

"No flag. No allegiance. Pledges proved unsafe in a confluence of secret societies and spies," Tobias noted. Then he added, "It appears that this necklace has a twin. One side is convex, while the other is flat with metallic insertion pegs. I bet that the other half it is buried six feet under, probably with a Tory."

"With a few exceptions, something held those who fought together, otherwise the nation would not have made it this far," Joan surmised. "That's why I say personal relationships played a major role in the American Revolution."

"Yes, I agree," Tobias said softly. "Personal relationships would be important to any trader on the spice route. This is where our story on the Eagle's Flight begins. According to the light of the crystal, a great place to begin would be an ashram in India. The year would be about 1769, six years before she died."

"That makes sense, given the theme of transcendence coursing through the fragmented story lines," Joan told him. "Sleep on it, Tobias. I'm sure you'll have your story tomorrow."

Chapter Two

Without trust

Without friends

Life might as well have had me

Satisfy the appetite of a lion

But, there wasn't a lion big enough in India

So I was forced to go to New England

For the revolution that began

In 1775

Reference Tune: *Jet Liner*

----Steve Miller Band

BENGAL, INDIA, 1769

"THIS PLACE IS going to the jungle," Susan told the swami with the turban.

"Yes, the United East India company is having the natives uproot their food crops and plant opium," he remarked. "One out of every three people will die from starvation. Untended property gets claimed by the surrounding forests."

Susan looked around at the high density populace. She estimated, "That will bring the genocide count to almost ten million. I am concerned about the effect on the spice trade."

"The coffers of the British East India Company will probably suffer, while their bankers in India grow rich," the swami told her. "I saw it in my meditation this morning. Your family should get out of the country."

"My family has been selling spices to the company for five generations," Susan protested.

"Hitch a ride on one of those ships bound for America," he suggested. "Your time here is limited."

"What do you mean by that?" Susan asked.

"I saw that in the meditation, too," he replied. "Remember that in India, time moves in circles, almost like a spiral. In the West, people pass their time like it is a line."

Puzzled by the time differences, Susan studied the ground underneath her bare feet. When she looked up, she saw that the swami had vanished in the crowd. Smiling to herself, she recognized this phenomenon as business as usual. Now you see 'em; now you don't. She, herself, had learned how to disappear in a crowd, though perhaps not as swiftly as the seasoned swami.

Noticing an Indian boy running toward her, she waited a few steps away from where she had stood with the seated swami. He instructed her in a hushed voice, "Your older brother wants you to come home quickly. It is important."

"What is going on?" she asked, following her companion across the busy street.

"All the swamis in the country are gathering at the nearby ashram. They are concerned about the ships," he said. "Your brothers are going to fight them."

"Ships?" she questioned. Peering above the crowd at the waterfront, she observed, "I see no problems on the dock."

"The ones in the sky," he said, pointing at some gray cigar-shaped objects hiding in the clouds.

"Not them again!" she cried.

"Here, your brother told me to give you this," he said, thrusting a necklace in her hands. "It will protect you."

"It is the necklace that my father gave him before he died. It had belonged to the father of my great-grandfather. He had it made when they formed the knighthood with the adepts of the head swami. Together they forged a route with the descendants of Marco Polo. After, the snake-worshipping marauders on the Silk Road killed three of his wives, he networked with the Brahmins. They liked him. Though he only had one wife, they always targeted the native women that he wed." Then, looking down at the necklace in her hands, as if it contained parting instructions, she said, "People regrouped easily in those days."

"Many wives, many masters," her friend said, nodding his head firmly.

"I'll try to remember that," she said, breaking out in a run.

She raced past her friend on the street. A lightning bolt erupted from the clouds, and sections of the busy city caught fire. Looking ahead in the distance, she saw that her brother's house engulfed in flames. Turning her head toward a hillside on the horizon, she saw that the ashram had vanished. People around her were emerging into nothingness with a pop. She watched her companion disappear as his mouth opened widely, gasping more in bewilderment than fear. Accepting his demise, he slowly became invisible to her.

Only a few steps away, she found her neighbor writhing in pain on the ground. The neighbor lived a few houses down from the one she shared with her brother, the last of her three older siblings. Long ago, her father had passed the necklace to the surviving men in the family. No one was left of her past relationships now, except for the wife of the impoverished trader. Glancing at the necklace in her hands before rushing toward the woman with the ebony eyes and long, dark hair, she wondered whether the necklace served to keep them both on this plane of existence. She reached for the woman and held the crystal against her light-brown shoulder. Her convulsions ceased immediately. Looking up at Susan with glistening black eyes, she quivered slightly as beads of perspiration formed on her forehead.

Stooping over the recovering body, Susan felt a sharp twinge in her lower back. Apparently, she had been injured. The exact nature of the wound perplexed her. She reasoned that it had something to do with the invisibility of the spiritually enlightened around her. Searching for answers inside the crystal of the necklace, she felt connected with forebears. She could visualize the face of the last wearer of the necklace. GO! His silent words mouthed at her. Then she recalled the chattering of the swami, which struck her profoundly. Hitch a ship.

Realizing her next move, she straightened her back and helped the woman to her feet. Unfortunately, she had become an invalid sometime in the last fifteen minutes since the alien attack and the crack in the time continuum. Susan paused for a moment. Somewhere, sometime ago, she sensed that she had experienced a similar disaster in another place in time. Knowing deep within herself that she could not separate from her neighbor, she searched her environment for the most peaceful, unaffected landmark in the area. Above the confusion and commotion, she spied a privateer ship in calm waters at an isolated harbor.

First we raid the till at the shop, then we pay for passage with the privateers, Susan thought. Visualizing her steps before executing them, she began dragging the woman towards the ship about three hundred yards away. Close your eyes and go to sleep, Susan instructed the woman in a foreign tongue. Without any further messaging, the woman did as directed, lapsing into a semiconscious state. She looked down at the woman, who did not have any place left to go. Determined to make her ride as easy and as comfortable as possible, Susan decided to go directly to the privateers. Her experience in retail would prove handy as she negotiated such parameters with them. When she entered the view of the men working the dock, she waved for assistance. One of the men recognized her from his dealings with her brother's shop.

"We are cashing out," she told him. Then she split the necklace open and placed one half on the contentedly dozing woman. Susan found the Indian's newly found sense of peace reassuring as she tied the necklace securely around her neck. "By the way, where are you going?"

"America," he answered as he gracefully lifted the woman over one shoulder like a delicate sack of precious herbs and spices.

"Great," Susan decided. "She has family with the Indians there."

"Native Americans?" he questioned.

"You could call them that," Susan responded.

The man shrugged at her admission, agreeing with Susan that the woman's origins really were not their business. Having recognized the necklace from the Order of the Eagle guild, he accepted the stricken passenger, because the symbol represented those opposing human trafficking. Without a further word, he carried her away to her new quarters while summoning additional help to Susan's store.

"So you are the new owner," a man acknowledged when he saw her holding the necklace.

"Easy come, easy go," Susan commented.

Nodding his head, he followed her with his entourage to the shop located a quarter of a mile away. They walked briskly past smoldering buildings and injured people too far gone to recover. Taking a deep breath, Susan entered the store with the others behind her. She could feel the presence of the departed spirits of her brothers around her, and knew that she was doing the right thing. Whatever grief she held went away with their encouragement. Retrieving the books behind the counter, she quickly handed them over to the lead man, who had started to inventory the contents of the trading post. He was already familiar with the store from past business dealings.

Everything seemed in order, prepared in advance for an inevitable crisis. Emptying the place quickly, Susan left with the purchased contents, leaving the door unlocked in case a beggar came looking for shelter. The building no longer served her now; perhaps it could provide refuge for someone else. A new home could be a new life.

Aboard the privateer ship, the lead man directed her to the hold below the deck. She ducked her head beneath the thick planks of wood as she descended the stairs to find her neighbor. Sitting on the bare wooden floor beside the reclined woman, Susan took a deep breath as she collected her thoughts. The woman eyes flickered while remaining motionless on a bedroll that had been stretched out for her. Relieved to find that the woman still seemed oriented in her new surroundings, Susan offered no plan or explanation. She knew that no words were necessary for those who traveled lightly through life. Instead, Susan lightly smirked as if to say well, here we are. The woman's eyes moistened in response, and a light smile tugged at the corners of her lips. Any place seemed better than the hell that they had left.

Studying the omniscient face of the woman, Susan noticed the signs of dehydration. She looked up to figure out where she might replenish the nearby flask. While Susan sat near the lying woman, a man suddenly appeared from behind the cargo boxes and greeted her. Having anticipated her next move, he handed her a jug of fresh water. Slightly alarmed by the masculine presence, Susan's neighbor stirred uncomfortably.

"Major John Andre," he introduced himself. "I am not really a major yet, but I intend to convince the King of England to commission me. For the moment, I am just doing the work of a major in India."

He remained standing, towering over the women on the floor of the ship. Susan poured some water for her neighbor to sip, and held the cup steady as the woman leaned forward to grasp the container with both hands. Trembling from weakness and trauma, she composed herself sufficiently enough to quench her thirst. Then she collapsed back down on the bedroll, and stared at the man with wide eyes.

"I watched you drag her across the streets to the boat. How old are you?" he asked pointedly.

"Eleven," Susan replied, studying the man closely. Now she became the one observing his every move. "Why didn't you help?"

"I was busy running for my life," he told her. "How old is your neighbor?"

"I think she is about twenty," Susan estimated. "Her husband traded herbs and spices with my older brother. I've seen her around the store on various occasions."

"You are one of the Eagles," he commented.

"Yes, my brothers told me that there had been female knights. They prepared me to carry out the mission when they passed over. Now that the

Silk Road has been destroyed and seized by dark occultists, it is left to the Eagles to protect commerce on the Spice Route."

The presence of the ship's captain interrupted their chit-chat. He wore a similar necklace over his heart. Carrying a tray, the captain offered steaming hot cups of spice milk to the passengers.

"I am sorry about the loss of your brother and related family," he began. "Luckily, you figured out how to work with the Eagle sunstone. Some people call it the king's stone, because they often used in the past to reflect on important decisions. That's how you made your way out of the alien attack, escaped the time aberration, and found your way to our ship."

"I also had help from a swami and a friend," Susan confessed. "I saw them minutes before the ambush on the sacred temple."

Both men sat down on some nearby crates as they savored the beverage. The room remained dark except for some streaks of daylight pouring down the stairwell. The major lit an oil lamp and continued with their discussion.

"I can use your help with the ship," the captain told Susan. "Come help me with the helm at dusk. We leave the dock in an hour. The major and his traveling companion can take turns nursing your neighbor back to health. What made you decide to drag her with you?"

"After seeing everything that I loved about my home in India disappear or go up in smoke, I wanted to bring something from my past with me to the New World. She responded to the Eagle crystal and came along willingly, almost seemed happy about leaving. The India that we once knew is gone now. It will take hundreds of years for it to return, if it ever does. For generations, my family has cultivated the spices of life and passed them along to the world. I would hate to see their work disappear. I would hate to see the aliens win and turn the world into gray, eliminating the colors of the rainbow." Teary eyed, Susan continued as her neighbor eagerly nodded as if she understood every word said. "Her father is native Indian. Her mother came from the British, the ones who worked with Marco Polo to establish safe commerce on the Silk Road. All her life, she has been between two worlds, accepted only by the Eagles and the spiritual elite of India. I think that is why the king's stone resonated with her. As for me, I have this penchant for working with whatever life drops in front of me." Pausing for a moment, Susan dried her tears and examined the contents of a large chest that she had saved for herself. She added, "My brothers prepared the chest for emergencies. It contains seeds for the cultivation of prize herbs and spices. Some are culinary. Others are medicinal. I understand that America is very fertile. I suspect that the plants that we love in India will grow well there."

"Great, I can help you set up shop in New England," the captain promised. "We can always use an establishment to sell our wares along with home-grown variety. It will lend stability to the operation."

"Meanwhile, I'll teach you how to shoot a musket," the major interrupted. "We must get past the pirates first. We have a long journey. These United India company flags get substituted for banners of skulls and bones at night."

"That is why we are out of port by dusk," the captain rejoined. "This city isn't getting any prettier."

Chapter Three

Both bonding and aloneness have their own unique issues

Reference Tune: *One*

----Three Dog Night

"WHERE IS YOUR traveling companion now?" Susan asked John Andre.

"He is sleeping in the captain's bunk," the man replied. "When he learns about the party in the hold, he'll probably want to make his quarters here."

The woman lying on the ground looked at the major with curiosity. Although she only spoke enough English for commerce, she understood much more through auditory channels. She had never considered her life a party, even less, hadn't known anyone that might envy it.

"Oh, speak of the devil," the ship's captain grinned. "Here comes our youngest passenger now."

In the gray shadows, the silhouette of a small boy could be seen making his way carefully down the stairs. He wandered to the group gathered around the reclining woman, and hopped into John Andre's lap. Smiling, he stared at the two females across from him. The neighbor eyed the scene and excitedly gesticulated at Susan. She expressed amazement to see such a young child wander confidently on the ship.

"The Duke of York is six years old," John Andre told them as he patted the boy's shoulders affectionately. "I rescued him from the Serpentine's boats; there may be hope for him yet. His father became mad enough to knight him at six months, and sent him to spy on the corporate pirates, who, of course, ambushed his ship at the same time they disrupted my yoga class at the ashram."

"The crew members call him Freddy," the captain piped. "However, in the presence of his father, we refer to him as Prince Frederick. The boy prefers being known as Freddy when he works as a privateer."

"So Freddy," John Andre began, looking down at his small pupil. "What are you going to report to your father about commerce in India now?"

"It's the Pitts," the boy acknowledged. "Lord Pitt and his group tried to sink me." Nodding firmly, he turned his head upward to address his teacher.

"Now Freddy, are we ever going to say this to the British Parliament?" the captain asked.

"Never," the boy answered. He seemed very excited about his new found secret. "The Prime Minister has a black heart."

"I think his father told him about the Prime Minister's health," John Andre mused.

"What color are hearts supposed to be?" the captain questioned.

"Red," Freddy announced.

"Yes, I think the king will be very happy to get his son back alive, especially when he recovers his senses," John Andre observed. "Tell your father that I will be very happy to be given a commission in Germany, one that is out of Pitt's reach." Then John Andre explained to Susan, "Like your neighbor, I am also between worlds. My father came from Switzerland, my mother came from France and birthed me in London. I am a merchant living with the English at a time when Pitt is chasing Frenchmen all over the continents."

"So Freddy, what do you think? Shall we drop these women off in New York before heading back home to the British palace?" John Andre queried. "It is on the way, and we'll need provisions. Perhaps a cup of hot chocolate to go?"

"Yes," Freddy agreed. "We'll drop them off after musket training. Let's take a bag of chocolate powder home from America." Then he brought his finger to his head, and contemplated a question for the major. "How old are you, Major John Andre?"

"I am nineteen," he told the boy. Then John Andre posed another question for Susan, "What is the name of your neighbor?"

"I don't know. I did not see her often," Susan admitted. "She seldom came to the store. My brothers were more acquainted with her husband. I don't think that they had been married long."

"What is your name?" Freddy asked, pointing to the brown-skin woman.

The neighbor intuited the meaning of Freddy's question. Pointing to herself, she said, "Shiva."

"Eva," Freddy repeated, dropping the sounds that he failed to pronounce correctly. He proudly said, "Eva."

After a brief glance at Susan, the all-knowing countenance of Shiva realized the limited vocabulary of the newly vocal youth, and resigned herself to the name change. Life seemed too short to argue, and the ethnic name might become a liability in a region where she would become a minority. Tossing her hair over one shoulder, she accepted the name change as a term of endearment. Instead, she pointed to a leather-bound journal tucked inside one of John Andre's pockets.

The major noticed the object of her attention, and retrieved his book for all to behold. "Oh, this," he said, placing the book in front of Freddy as he thumbed through a few pages. "Freddy and I will recite some poems that I have written. We'll entertain Eva while Susan and the captain find a safe way out of the harbor."

Eva nodded and smiled at her success in capturing the words of the major, who seemed only too delighted to share some of his soul with the group. Susan studied the dynamics; it appeared that the major wore his soul on his sleeve with his poetry collection. Occasionally she dabbled with written verses herself, but it represented more a connection with the divine. Susan played with verses, finding a wholeness or sense of completion within the act itself. Though she put her soul into her work, it did not necessarily represent her. She always stood apart from her words, allowing them to assume a life of their own and communicate never-ending revelations.

Meanwhile, the captain nudged Susan away from the hold. He climbed the stairs behind her slow steps. Horrified at the sight of the devastation greeting her when she reached the deck, she paused briefly as her low back muscles spasmed. Flames and smoke continued to engulf the large city, though there were no cries heard from the vanished. Recognizing that a poetry reading would have seemed too trivial for her under the circumstance, she resolved to pursue action rather than artful self-expression. Even under the most dire circumstances, Susan sought a time and place for everything. Her sensitivities directed her to assume control of her path in life.

"The wheel is over there," the captain pointed as he gently placed a firm hand on her shoulder. "There are two other ships leaving with us. Two of the king's vessels survived the attack. Now that they have identified their real enemies, they intend to depart with us. One of Freddy's cousins is aboard one of the remaining ships. We can help protect each other. There is safety in numbers, even in these dark waters."

Susan strode over to the helm. Taking a brief gulp of air, she cautiously placed her hands on the large circular steering device. She could feel the fullness of the ship underneath the weight of her palms. Somebody loosened the rope tying the ship to the dock, and Susan observed the motion of the boat in passing. The shadowy wooden planks of the pier went by her as the ship veered out to sea. The other two ships in the distance calmly followed. The captain put his hands next to hers, joining her at the big wheel. Too numb to cry, Susan watched the country that had been her former home, quickly submerge into the depths of the night. The moon had not risen yet. Black clouds overhead dimmed the stars in the sky to nothingness.

Turning her head westerly, Susan saw streaks of white lightning illuminate the lush mountains in the distance. She observed, "It's the Thunder People. We have protection from the alien sky ships. They are providing cover."

"Yes, our crystal necklaces transmitted our intentions to those willing to help," the captain commented. Reading the frequencies denoted by the flashing lights, he added, "They say that the cover will be short-lived. They can only offer temporary assistance. The aliens are watching closely for escapees."

Susan lightly gritted her teeth as she gripped the wheel. Searching for a swift current to propel them out of harm's way, she remarked, "It is better than nothing."

Chapter Four

I thought that you'd live forever
Your presence seemed so enduring

Reference Tune: *Flame*
----Cheap Trick

LATE IN THE night, John Andre appeared above deck and stood near the two at the helm. He surveyed the night air for landmarks on any far horizon. Without a word, he took several lengthy, deep breaths befitting a hearty practitioner of yoga and the Vedic arts. Then he turned to the pair frozen at the wheel, and studied their faces with his penetrating, dark wide-eyes.

"Eva's asleep finally. Freddy is tucked underneath her arm like a teddy bear. I think she is feeling maternal toward the boy. My poems eventually put to them to sleep, despite their resistance to give in to their fatigue. Mission accomplished, Captain," he reported with unemotional stiffness.

After another hour, the clouds left and a star studded sky lit the night's voyage. John Andre relieved Susan at the wheel. As she descended the stairs, she could hear the two men softly chatting amiably in dark. A small tear fell from her right eye, and she hurriedly brushed it away. Susan remembered the discussions of her older brothers in the evenings. They were advanced, having all been born under the constellation of Aquarius. Once she had overheard their manly voices fathom the madness of the British king.

"It's a condition due to stress-induced vitamin B deficiency," one brother said.

The other laughed, before adding, "We'll know all about vitamins 350 years from now. Maybe by then, people will understand the importance of diet and exercise. Imagine losing thirteen colonies due to a Vitamin B imbalance. It makes history."

With their lighthearted voices echoing in her memories, Susan carefully made her way to her present position in a hammock near the sleeping neighbor and princely foundling. A few stilled moments settled her body into a relaxed state, and the tension began to leave her. While in this abbreviated sense of rejuvenation, she heard Eva's muffled cries. Raising her head from the hammock, Susan searched in Eva's direction. She noticed the shadows of flailing arms, and hopped from the hammock to check on the reason. Leaning over Eva and the small boy, Susan detected a sense of alarm on her neighbor's tear-soaked face.

"Attack," she whispered in fear. "It is coming."

"Stay here," Susan instructed the woman. "I will tell the captain, and take a look on deck."

Relieved that she had been understood and her concerns heeded, Eva dried her tears and dropped back into her thoughts. The rest had regenerated Susan enough to point to where she could race up the stairs, while her mind remained calm, untouched by the hysteria of the weary. When she reached the deck, she saw a nearly full moon casting its quivering light through cloud breaks and lighting up the horizon. There, in the far distance she made out the forms of four British frigates closing in on the king's two ships. The moon disappeared behind cloud cover, and the frigates were hidden from view.

Susan approached John Andre, who had taken the wheel to relieve the captain's duty. He saw her coming, but remained silent, focused on his solitary work. As she neared the helm, the moon broke through the clouds briefly, providing a view of the silver half-human, half-fish forms, which dotted the waves to the east. Like the wind in the sails, her luck encouraged movement. Somehow she found immediate solutions to the problems presenting themselves.

Standing beside John Andre, she fixed her stare on the place where she had last spotted the frigates, and whispered, "We have company, and it isn't me. Eva foresaw an attack." Then she pointed into the black air. "Over there."

"Wake the crew. Summon the captain. I don't yet see what you both see, but I believe that it is time to get all hands and eyes on deck. I felt a chill run up my spine after I noticed that you had already risen from your short slumber." Deftly turning the wheel to the left he confessed, "As for Eva, her eyes will continue to haunt me for the rest of my life."

Susan did as John Andre recommended. Sensing the tension of the moment, the captain easily rose from his bunk. Donning his small telescope, he hurried to confer with his first mate, who also was rising to the occasion. Susan stopped and watched the crew come to life like ants learning about a picnic. Everyone rushed around wordlessly, and completed her task for her. Satisfied that they had stirred crew awake, she returned down the hold to inform Eva of her findings.

Sitting upright, Eva motioned for Susan's help in placing young into Freddy the hammock. He wiggled as they pushed and tugged him into a position for the move. His eyes flickered open for a few seconds, then he groggily closed them.

"Freddy, who gets to sleep in my bed now," Susan encouraged as she bundled him in a blanket for an artificial sense of security.

He succumbed to the sense of comfort without a word, and resumed resting. Meanwhile, Eva stood on her feet and swiftly attempted to ascend the stairs before anyone could stop her. Out of the corner of her eye, Susan watched her go, spending more time nestling Freddy to avoid her. When she spied the lower hem of Eva's dress escape her view, Susan paused for a few seconds and then quickly followed. Though alone, the safest place for Freddy on a fast moving ship remained tucked below, while every able body went above to bring the ship up to speed. Susan returned to the helm as if nothing seemed out of the ordinary.

"The captain has spotted the attack," John Andre confirmed in a low voice. His attention remained on navigating the vessel.

Noticing Eva bracing herself against a nearby rail, Susan ignored her and proceeded to partake in the activities around the ship's wheel.

"We'll have to fire a flare," the captain said quietly. "It doesn't look like they have spotted the frigates. Otherwise they would be moving much faster. We have no way to communicate with the king's vessels without betraying our presence. Might well light up the sky, and reveal our enemies. It will give them a chance to prepare for battle."

He gave hushed instructions to his first mate, who went to his quarters to retrieve a flare. Then he turned to Susan, "Your brother told me that you are a flame reader. Before we reveal ourselves, I want to know where to flee. One of the crew will light a lamp in my office, hidden from view of those at sea."

"Takes a flame to know a flame," John Andre, the eternal poet, murmured to himself as he tracked the speediest currents in the waters.

Susan scurried to the captain's office with the same crew member that had helped her board. Inside the walls of finished wood, the mate lit a hurricane lamp for Susan to study its flames. She watched the hues of yellow, blue, and orange reach for the height of the glass covering. Projecting her soul at the base of the multi-colored wick, she received confirmation for a solution that had been forming in her mind ever since appearance of the half-fish-half-human figures. She called them the merpeople. Like Andre and Eva, the merpeople inhabited two worlds. Once they had been readily visible to the human eye, but persecution had forced them to seek other dimensions. Convinced that they could lead the ship into a similar dimension, Susan examined the flicker for further details on how to enter this other dimension safely and emerge fully conscious and intact. She noticed that the dancing flame had its own rhythm, much like the waves that beat against the hull of the boat. They tracked that frequency and matched it to the waves of a particular current, which she knew could be detected on the horizon somewhere.

Stunned by the conclusions drawn from a single flame, Susan quickly told the mate to extinguish the lamp as she stepped outside the captain's quarters still mesmerized by the waving spectrum. Peering along the surface of the distant water, she centered on a section that reflected what she had just experience. When a stray moon beam illuminated the same section, she felt assured that they could find the protected health and happiness that had eluded them previously. Scouting the area with her analytical mind, she reasoned that such a path would not only send several images of the ship to confuse the pursuers, but would simultaneously hide them behind a cove consistent with the trajectory of the speeding frigate. They would have to turn around for a better look, which would lend itself to the escape of the king's ships.

Without calling attention to her, the captain waited for Susan's idealized concepts on his initial plan. When she turned toward the center from the ship's edge, he stopped her. He didn't focus on her directly, so that she would comfortably speak her mind. He wanted to see what she had intuited, and searched the horizon for inspiration.

"I get that if we send the flare when the ship hits that region a quarter mile away to the east, the light will bounce off the moon, clouds, and mountains. The corporate frigates will view several images. By the time they decide on the correct one, the freshwater current from that land side waterfall will bring the ship around the cove and out of sight." Spending a moment to inhale the salt air in favor of the freshwater aroma emerging from the upcoming waterfall, she asked the captain, "How many cannons do we have?

"Four, at best," he admitted. He sighed and lightly shrugged his shoulders. "One of the mates counted ten a piece for the king's ships, which are twice the size of ours. The frigates have eight cannons, though they're twice as fast as the heavier king's ships. We are merchants, not fighter ships or royal diplomats. We get by on a wealth of personal relationships."

"What can I do to help now?" Susan asked.

"Stay focused on your merpeople," he advised. "I'll take care of the rest."

He left to give further instruction to the crew and sent John Andre below deck along with Eva. Susan studied the beautiful luminous forms swimming in front of the ship, seeming to guide it out of the chaos behind. For a moment, she turned around and watched the first mate aim the flare in the sky. Then she faced the water again. The merpeople had disappeared as a brilliant light exposed whatever had sought refuge in the dark shadows. A shock of fear ran up her spine, and she concentrated on the beautiful peace she had once enjoyed feeling. Seconds later, cannon fire erupted from the pursuing frigates. The king's ships wasted no time in returning the fire, the result of being served by highly trained military personnel. However, the element of surprise paralyzed the response of the king's ships. The crown hesitated to be aggressive towards those considered subjects. The corporate frigates were more earnest in their attack, and soon the king's ships were engulfed in flames. Apparently, they intended to destroy witnesses rather than seize prizes, knowing that Freddy's esteemed cousin piloted the largest ship of the skirmish. The frigates drifted away from the sinking vessels without pursuing the merchant ship, which vanished behind the fog emanating from the mists of the cove.

Chapter Five

If you feel a pang

Streaking across your heart

When someone is gone

Then you know for certain

Without doubt

That you knew love

Maybe it wasn't really them,

But it was love all the same

Reference Tune: *Love Hurts*

----Nazareth

"THE MULTI-DIMENSIONAL WORK gave us enough time to escape the attack," the captain told Susan as they speedily hurried away from the fog. "It is not enough to heal or reverse the negative cycle because we have too many irons in the fire, so to speak."

"The best that we could do for the moment would be to create a win-win situation," Susan agreed. "No advancement or development, though it appears that we can get past the loss."

"We must remain cautious as we sail around the world," the captain observed. "We witnessed a major power play. I have a feeling that the crown will not step up to the plate and respond to the attack. As usual, they will blame pirates for the death of the royal."

"The life of a privateer is private enterprise, free from royal or parliamentary corporate influence," Susan commented.

"If irritated enough, privateers become thieves," the captain stated. "I suspect that both the crown and the corporate strings on the puppet parliament do not want another Robin Hood of their own creation. The world is much bigger as a result of Marco Polo's excursions. Instead of Robin Hoods, we have revolutions in the making. Robin Hood, his life partner, and merry men were all descendants of Welsh, Irish, English, and Scottish royalty. Their descendants eventually brought fugitives from the House of Spencer to the New World; their quarrel is not with their parents. The conflicts are with those who pursue their parents, and why their parents remain complacent."

Susan left the deck and went below with her thoughts concerning the discussion with the captain. Everyone was asleep in the hull. Freddy remained curled in the hammock. She grabbed a spare wool blanket and created a makeshift bedroll on the floor behind the cargo boxes. Relaxing on the wood floor of the hull, Susan reflected on the events of the evening. Daylight would arrive in a few hours. After fifteen minutes, she decided to return to the deck. She could not rest. The finality of the burning, sinking ships seared the memories of her older brothers. The captain with his newfound necklace, which had been given to him by a dying knight, linked her to her brothers. Wiping a few stray tears, she pushed the loneliness away, and decided to greet the sunrise. She felt more comfortable dozing on the deck. These nighttime conversations always starkly entered her consciousness like a fast moving fresh water stream that rapidly polished the edges of things she thought she knew. She found that these moments refined not only her world view, but her own definition of self. Though these moments never amounted to a rude awakening, it was always the inevitable rudeness of the awakening that stoked the embers within to a fire that she could not ignore. Like the burning of the ships, she witnessed the conflagration inside herself and did nothing but run with it. As she climbed the stairs back to the salty air, she accepted her passion as a dear friend. Pausing briefly at the top, Susan observed the ever-changing scene and realized that this passion could carry her past her grief with its life-giving, though painful transmutation.

The captain and crew came and went, changing positions while taking different shifts to make sure everyone had a chance to rest and recover. Susan wedged herself in a secure seat on the wooden floor before tying herself to a nearby iron cleat. She didn't want to stay awake enough to realize the effect of what had previously transpired. A light doze in an altered state suited her best for the moment. The motion of people around her proved grounding. By the time the sun cast red and orange hues and beams over the horizon to the far reaches of the ship, she realized that she had left India behind in the frothy wake. The surrounding blue green waves comforted her with a womb-like presence.

She maintained this warm sense of isolation in the months that followed. There were daily exercises in musket training conducted by John Andre and the crew member that had helped her board. After fully regaining her health, Eva joined the musket practice, while little Freddy learned reading skills through poetry assignments under the major's tutelage. People pitched in to help with the various chores, while the ship collected livestock and sundries at ports along the way. Sometimes they traded their goods. The ship operated like a moving store, satisfying customers across the globe in worthwhile commerce.

One crew member decided to keep a cow for himself. He taught Susan how to milk her, and she appropriated the task after the cow bonded under the spell of her handiwork. Susan learned that cows could also be good friends. Everyone on the ship came to see the cow as a friend for many reasons. Someone named her Matilda, and the cow responded, seeming to know the words of those around her.

When they docked at Cape Horn, Susan had another searing discussion with the captain. As earlier, the moment crept upon her without any awareness. He sought her while the ship's crew conducted the usual port business. However, Susan noticed that the ship kept an unusual distance from the town and out of view from the corporate slave ships. Curious, she wondered why the captain considered the town a threat. The presence of the ships dealing openly in human trafficking concerned her. Obviously, they had support of the natives.

Perceptive to changes in the weather and waves as well as privy to the inclinations of those on board his ship, he approached her once she assumed a more visible position on deck, having left a reserved, guarded position behind one of the oak pillars. Making eye contact, she warmed to his approach. As if they were in their own little world, he began another discussion she would never forget.

"We are staying away from the commercial side of this town," he confided, having guessed her innermost thoughts.

Relieved that he would address her inquiry, she waited for him to proceed.

"The neighbors of the natives are sold for their land," he added.

Aghast by his pointed analysis of the situation, she slightly wavered in her stance. The detached, soft eyes of the captain's eyes steadied her. Without calling attention to her shock, he related his interpretation of the present circumstances.

"What we witnessed in India was only a result of a global problem," the captain explained without a trace of panic or fear.

"Is this why the crew refers to this place as the Dark Continent?" she asked.

"Yes. It is so dark, that we forgot why we called it that," he answered, brightening at her astuteness. "It really has nothing to do with the color of one's skin. Your next job is to avoid being detected along with Eva and little Freddy. I won't be able to afford to buy all three of you back at once."

Briefly, they smiled wryly at each other. Then Susan joined Eva, who ushered Freddy toward the company of Matilda below deck. They nodded at each other with the understanding that both had received the captain's message. Before dropping into the hold, Susan glanced at the serious expression on the face of bustling crew members. They were heavily arming themselves for the looming business transactions in town.

"Let's show Matilda our muskets," Susan suggested in a manner to avoid alarming Freddy.

"Yes, our muskets," Eva agreed, bending over Freddy to help him collect his wit.

The young boy firmly grasped the need for self-defense without any further explanation. He also had seen his favorite crew members don weapons they used strictly for training purposes. The practice was over. A shooting pain seeming streaked across his heart with the sense of tragedy, perhaps loss of innocence associated with the reality of commerce with a dark continent.

Susan reached for her musket and held it firmly in her hands. The gun distinguished her from the natives. She waved Eva and Freddy on toward the stalls in a section away from the sleeping quarters. Peering out a tiny window across the harbor, she imagined what her brothers might say about African slave trade.

They trade their neighbors, and seize their land. Three-hundred-fifty years from now, their old neighbors will have created a new family of soul brothers and sisters in the New World. Their former neighbors will have learned spiritual expression and community, while their country will be taken by the same corporation with whom they do business.

Peering through the tiny portal, Susan noticed a British frigate moving their way. She looked up at the daylight shining through the stairwell and saw the captain quietly garnering a select group of crew. He directed them to various strategic positions hidden behind wooden structures on the ship. Now she understood why he had confided in her, before sending her to the hold.

His gaze fell down the passage and their eyes met. He always seemed to sense when she needed him, even if it was just for a glance. Satisfied that she held a firm grasp on the moment, he lightly brought his hand to the eagle necklace as if invoking another escape. The projection worked, and she found the light reflected in her own piece. Then they left each other.

Susan walked swiftly to the stall at the far end; she found Eva holding Freddy on one knee as they consulted Matilda. Matilda turned her head toward Susan without offering the typical moo. For once, the cow was keeping her comments to herself.

"We have company," Susan whispered. "Let's build a fort with the bales of hay."

Eva shot Susan a look of terror, and Susan noticed a slight shudder run down the spine of her milk cow. Freddy ignored the two. Hopping off Eva's lap, he tried pushing a bale with his small hands.

"Here, let me give you a hand with that," Susan interjected. Putting her musket safely aside, she joined Freddy's efforts. She asked him, "Where should we put it?"

"Over there," he stopped, standing erect. Sizing up the quarters, he pointed and stated. "They won't see us if we put it over there."

"That looks good to me," Susan said as she situated the bale with an extra push from Eva.

After rearranging the hay, they ducked behind separate rows of straw across from each other. If an intruder found one person, then the others would have a chance to shoot the attacker in the back. Everyone kept steady watch on the entrance to the stall. They heard the gunfire break out, though no cannons fired. Heavy footsteps pelted the floor above like thunder.

Forty minutes later, the captain came downstairs and spoke to Matilda while they emerged slowly from their straw barriers.

Standing upright with a wounded left hand over his chest to slow the bleeding, he talked into the air as if making a general announcement. "It is safe to come out. We have another boat. The former inhabitants spent too much time drinking last night. We have good karma with our neighbors."

Freddy bounced from his hiding position and approached the captain. Looking up, he saluted the man. The tall, man in his early fifties laughed and smiled at the small boy. Leaning over the lad, he picked him up while being careful to avoid aggravating his injured forearm. For a few seconds he grimaced as he connected with the pain, but a heart-warming grin filled his countenance.

"What about a cup of spice tea?" he asked young Freddy.

Chapter Six

Sorry isn't everything

Sometimes sorry isn't anything

But words for some people

Reference Tune: *Hard To Say I'm Sorry*

----Chicago

DIVIDING THE CREW passengers between the two ships, the captain instructed them to brace for an upcoming wind storm. Susan, Eva, and John Andre went to the faster frigate, while Freddy stayed in the company of the captain who assumed full responsibility for the king's son. The king's close advisors had been notified of his son's survival, and had sent a flotilla of fifty ships to escort his safe return. The royal Navy was coming straight from England to Cape Horn. Their estimated arrival loomed only two days away.

The owner of Matilda captained the ship, which had been acquired as booty. They dubbed it the new ship in honor of their destiny in the new world. Everything on the new ship appeared bigger, more efficient, and less weathered. There was even a tiny window in Matilda's stall, and the milk cow appreciated turning her snout in the emanating sunbeams.

In the evening, the treacherous breeze erupted into a fierce gale, sweeping saltwater over the upper deck. Occasionally, some water spilled over into the hold, down the staircase. As usual, the remaining three retired to the hold, while the ship's crew pieced their way across the ship. This time, Susan fell asleep to the sound of bellowing wind, blowing changes in the pre-measured threads of their lives. She knew some would be more affected than others.

The storm ended by morning. Susan awoke relatively late for her personal pattern, and was greeted by the sight of a new dawn crystallizing in the tiny dewdrops forming on the ropes dangling from various posts above. Eva hovered in the corner, surveying the calm sea as a backdrop against the havoc of the past night. The captain at the wheel excitedly motioned Susan to focus her attention on the broken main mast. The captain on the broken boat waved at Susan as the distance between them gradually increased. He, in turn, directed her attention to the appearance of the royal navy on the horizon. Susan looked at the wheel on her own ship. The new captain nodded at her. They were going on to England, while the other ship would stay behind for repairs with a segment of the navy.

"The captain is accompanying Freddy home. They will repair his ship in his absence," he told her, seeming to anticipate her question.

Susan watched the captain on the opposite ship instruct Freddy on the importance of swabbing the upper deck. The new ship had already been cleared from the storm's debris, while the much slower ship waited for assistance from the royal navy. She noted the expression of relief on the face of the captain, who clasped the necklace over his chest while continuing to find entertainment for Freddy.

Her attention turned to the new captain. His hands steadied on the helm and he told her, "You can call me Marcus. I want your help as a navigator."

Susan blinked at him. For now the ship belonged to them, not John Andre, not the prince, or the fugitive from India still wrapped in an oppressive culture. The captain mentioned once that Marcus was eighteen years old, only a year younger than John Andre. Though they never said much, except through songs cheerfully sung as they worked the ropes on deck together, Marcus and Susan stayed in tune with each other's thoughts.

Holding the necklace in her hand, Susan searched the horizon and noted the reflection in the light shining through the layers of the crystal. She pointed to the different features, explaining to Marcus, "Let's keep a day's distance from the royal navy. All indications suggest that they are not trustworthy."

Marcus nodded, turning the wheel around. Her instructions confirmed his suspicions. John Andre would not be particularly happy about the route, having intended to use his association with Freddy to gain admission into the king's armed forces. The teenage captain looked forward to some free-sailing without the troublesome prince aboard. He had worn out his welcome, only appearing adorable to Eva, who evaluated her self-worth in child-rearing terms. Like the seasoned members of the crew, Susan and Marcus kept their bearings on the big picture, while some drowned in misery without realizing it. They held their tempers, forging tolerance for the misguided world authority. Maintaining balance under the circumstances, Susan and Marcus cultivated an inner sense of freedom.

Despite all his yoga practice, John Andre never got the message. He served as a remnant of the entrapped enlightened left behind in India. For Susan, the presence of her brothers seemingly became more powerful in their absence, as if she had never really lost them. Like an ocean, her perception of this fine detail was expanding. In comparison, John Andre and Eva wandered like souls buried at sea by their loss, neither here, there, or in-between. Unable to realize what they had, they lost everything to the sea, which consumed any reflective trace of belonging.

Recognizing that Eva and John Andre evolved into born losers by the constant stream of prose that they elicited from each other, the crew fathomed that perpetual angst served as an anchor locking an individual to the murky depths. Such leadership was not to be entertained, much less engaged. The ship's inhabitants focused their sights on the great wheel in the sky above, sailing above the waves. Unfortunately, Eva and John Andre, like Freddy, missed the boat metaphorically.

Though the ship's crew pursued one narrow escape after the other, they gradually became invisible to life's vicissitudes. Instead of focusing on the ups and downs, they steadied themselves and lived life to the fullest. In this manner, judgment passed on the living and dead. There were those like Eva and John Andre, who consisted of the walking dead, and those similar to Susan's brothers, who appeared to have greater lives in their departure.

Staring into the waves as she breathed the salt air, Susan recalled the lighthearted projections of her brothers.

Two hundred years from now, some guy is going to bring up this point after a terrible civil war battle. Amidst the corpses strewn all around him in a place in America called Getty-something, he will hammer this point home about judging the living and dead. It is a critical evolution of a mission here and now.

Like the grains of sand on the ocean floor, Susan's understanding became more refined under theses wavy conditions, which she could not simply sidestep on the boat. Meanwhile, the intellectualization of individual libidinous fantasies, through the skillful arrangement of words, quickly staled on the hard-working crew, who learned that it was best to leave Eva and John Andre alone and not solicit their help, particularly in critical moments. Actions did not suit the group, which had whittled down to a twosome after the departure of the loafing prince. Secure in the rarified atmosphere above the hold, Susan felt protected from the poison contaminating Eva and Andre in a world epidemic of wannabes.

"Wanna be night watch?" Marcus asked the next week.

"Maybe for a day," she answered.

"That's not funny," he said with a grin. "Night watch is at night."

Dodging his request, she asked, "Who else is staying up?"

"I think there was another crew member, one who sidelines as a night owl," Marcus reflected, cocking his head side to side thoughtfully.

"Oh, he's staying up," interjected a crew member who happened to wander into the conversation. "I'll stay up."

"Me, too," another wandering crew member interjected. He eagerly nodded his head.

"Might as well make a party of it," Susan observed, stepping back from the group a bit.

"No one will sleep except Eva," a third crew member remarked. "Maybe we can entice John Andre to join us for a moment."

This is how affairs were conducted without the former captain. It was hard to say that they were sorry for the circumstances or ensuing misunderstandings. Under the steady hands of the young leaders, the workload transformed into play. That described life aboard a small vessel, either work together in the same rhythm or become overwhelmed by discord. Bearing silent axes to grind, Eva and John Andre chose the latter experience of disharmony, which marked their sad destinies. Eva would eventually come to find what she wanted, only to lose it without ever coming to fruition. John Andre simply would remain unfortunate. Meanwhile, the others flew like eagles, finding the opportunities in chaos. Like her brothers, the crew's transcendent heartiness compelled them to fully enjoy themselves during the worst of times, and they remained untouched by their enemies through the subtle light they brought to the world.

Rolling with the psychological waves of despair and hope, the captured frigate breezed into the tideway known as the Pool of London. Marcus efficiently docked the ship on one of the wharves selected by Susan and unloaded their cargo. Though isolated from the busiest section of town, the new ship was soon surrounded by gawkers. Word quickly spread around town concerning the curios hawked by the sailors. Several of their favorite merchants greeted the ship after they recognized the crew.

"Nice frigate," one bearded vendor remarked as Marcus tossed him a forty pound bag of tea. "Where did you find it?"

"The wind blew it our way," he said with a twinkle in his eye.

The vendor laughed. Then he said, "I want one."

"You'll have to wait for the captain's arrival," Marcus acknowledged. "We expect him in a month."

"How about a stout for you and your navigator with the eagle necklace?" another vendor offered. "We need to talk, but not until I get my goods off your ship." Then he handed Marcus an address with cash for the inventory. "At the dark of the moon tonight."

Susan admired the handshake Marcus extended heartily to the man who had paid him. Looking up at her as the man departed quietly down the pier, Marcus raised the money in the air in a congratulatory salute and beamed confidently. Their celebration was short-lived as two uniformed emissaries from the royal family approached the ship. Susan dashed behind a thick wooden beam to watch the interaction between them and Marcus to avoid undue notice.

With a little polite stomp, one of the uniformed men handed Marcus an official-looking piece of parchment. "Orders for John Andre. We have been informed that he is aboard your ship. King George III has appointed him captain of a regiment in Germany in appreciation of his support. Where can we find him?"

"He's on board gathering his things," Marcus answered. Without calling attention to Susan, he summoned a crew mate. "Please tell John Andre that the king's men are awaiting him."

Then he turned to the officers and said without any hint of emotion, "He has been expecting you. He'll be here soon."

Moments later, John Andre appeared before the king's men. He studied the parchment they purveyed with a light smile. Then he lifted his pack to his shoulder and accompanied the men off the ship. Several of the crew followed behind with his belongings neatly tucked away in wooden crates. As they left the ship, Marcus stacked a wooden box to shield Susan and him from view in case they decided to look back. Susan stepped away from the wooden beam and stood beside him as he rested. A stray member of the crew joined them.

Together they gazed at the wordless passing of the man who had spent almost a year with them on a treacherous voyage. No one said good-bye. Watching John Andre make his way off the boat, the stray crew member observed, "He's going to hang with the Loyalists."

Subtle shocks of recognition raised the brow of Marcus, and Susan curiously watched his reaction to the double meaning of the word hang. He walked away from his position and pondered the reliability of the company that had carried John Andre away. Going into his office to complete further business, he nodded quietly and left them alone. Susan stared a few seconds at the shipmate, who met her gaze with a sense of bewilderment. Then he handed her a few of the smaller crates and they completed the tasks on deck with the others.

When the night appeared most black, Susan found the captain outside his quarters. Having donned a cloak to conceal his sailor's attire, he ushered her silently off the boat. They climbed down a ladder at the far end of the ship and hopped down on an uninhabited section of the older, weathered dock. They stole their way through town unnoticed by late night strollers. Making their way into a pub, they opened the door to a warmly lit room. There were only a few people left at the bar. The vendor motioned for them to join his table, while the owner acknowledged their presence with an offhand gesture.

Sitting down at the table after Susan, Marcus quietly began, "What is the news about the Green Dragons in Boston?"

From lessons learned from her brothers, Susan knew that the Green Dragons enlisted as soldiers, whereas the eagles served as their intelligence.

"Well, they have a tavern, but that's about it," the vendor answered. "Penn's patriots have started military training, while the Loyalists have seized the reigns of the royal family. The Tories are beckoning to Parliament for guidance, while dark occultists are playing the native Cherokees against the different colonial factions. The French Indian War has left the region in total chaos. It doesn't look good for anyone, much less the continents."

"Yes, the aliens and their warships blasted our commercial interests in India. We have to regroup. Susan and a few others are going to start a co-op in Concord to get a hold on the winery business amongst other things."

The vendor sipped his mulled cider before raising his glass in a mock toast, "Gaud knows that we need something to drink. Rumor has it that the patriots plan to contaminate the water supply on the New England coast."

"Gaud?" Susan questioned.

"Outerspace sponsors for our civilizations on earth," Marcus explained. "Unfortunately, they didn't make it, though we still invoke them out of respect for our beginnings."

"I hear that they almost murdered the Duke of York," the vendor interrupted, wishing to keep focused.

"He never was safe under the tutelage of his moody father," Marcus commented. "They downed his cousin. The king's armies need to be reorganized and reformed. He is a little bit young for that now."

The conversation stopped when they heard a loud thud from the bartender dropping a glass on the counter.

"That's our cue," the vendor observed. "Back to the ship you two. My workpeople can load you in the dark. When they finish, moor at the far end of the harbor. Minimize your presence here until the captain arrives."

Time passed without any further events after they left the scene at the pub. They heeded the vendor's advice and conducted commerce only at nightfall. The king's men provided minimal protection, sensing that the frigates would be numbered as soon as they left the harbor. Focusing on their business pursuits, the crew entertained the notion that there was nowhere else to go but to New England.

The captain sailed his ship unceremoniously to the wharf and met the king's men. Seeing his return from afar, Marcus opted for one last docking to confer with the captain. They tied the frigate to the posts as the uniformed men came to whisk young Freddy away.

Eva appeared on deck for the moment and stood with Susan as they waved farewell to Freddy. The youngster raised his hand and greeted the crew as they wished him well. Freezing in his steps, he turned suddenly and astutely studied the presence of the officers around him. The prince raised his head and whiffed the aroma hanging over the port. Then he ordered the king's men, "Go home." Quickly turning on his heels, he ran straight to the frigate where Eva stretched out her arms. Marcus seized the moment and quickly undid the ropes. Freddy jumped on board before the officers could make up their minds. Burying his face in the arms of Eva and Susan, he promised to behave.

"I'll be good," he cried. "I want to go with you. Please don't leave me."

Marcus set sail for America, while the captain smiled his approval. He discreetly motioned for the crew to help without calling attention to their actions.

"He wants to visit his cousins in New England," he explained to the gaping uniformed men. The ship drifted out to sea as he spoke. "It's a family affair. We are on a tight schedule."

A few of the former crew members climbed aboard the emptied boat. Highly skilled at reading emergency situations, minds, and sign language, they had already made their way to the ship once Marcus gave them the go-ahead. The ship drifted away from the dock as the captain excused himself from the departing officers, who did not want to further complicate their lives with further interventions. The captain nodded his agreement with their complacency, "Say hello to his Mom for me. I understand that the king is on vacation. We'll be back soon. See you."

Chapter Seven

It's a shrewd life

Reference Tune: *St. Elmo's Fire*

----John Parr

A STRONG WIND blew the two ships out of the harbor. Everyone, including Freddy worked hard to bring both ships to full speed. Nobody pursued them for the moment. The frigate led the way across the waters, while the captain's ship followed a quarter mile behind. America loomed as their next destination.

When Freddy began to grow weary, Eva took the youngster below deck for a cup of chai. Susan remained at the wheel and scanned the horizon for royal or corporate ships. Occasionally, she climbed to the crow's nest for a better look. Having divided the crew between two ships, there was no one to spare. When nightfall came, Eva and Susan took turns sleeping beside Freddy, who required a full night's rest in a quiet area. For his part, Freddy adjusted to the routine and successfully cut his sleep time short. He learned how to become invisible on deck, lending an eager hand as if he had been born on a boat. The rest of the skeleton crew decided their own rotation schedule, one that best suited them for balancing activity with rest.

By the fourth night of the journey, Eva felt compelled to rouse Susan from her rest. Awaking in the pitch darkness, Susan blinked and raised her head. Freddy stirred in the bunk above hers. A streak of light soared above them and briefly lit the expression of terror on Eva's face. Susan slowly lowered her head as some muffled booms resonated in the background. Hopping out of bed, she reached for Freddy in the eerie blackness that followed.

"C'mon, Freddy," she gently told him. Without a hint of panic in her voice, she told him, "We must swim for it. Something tells me that things are already too far in motion to stay."

Eva heard Susan's words, and gathered some belongings. She grabbed Susan's chest of seeds along with several knapsacks, which had been pre-packed for quick departures. Giving their resting quarters one last glance, Eva swerved on her heels and hurried after Susan.

"Swim?" Freddy asked in a hush voice.

Susan held his hand in hers and encouraged him up the stairs.

"Yes, like whales," she replied. "If we are lucky, then maybe one will take out the ship that's attacking us."

"Hmm," Freddy pondered out loud as he stepped his way to the top. Flames erupted from the darkness behind them. The sound of rushing water filled the air amidst the thunder of cannon fire.

"Keep thinking about the whales," Susan instructed. "Meanwhile, it's time to get off this burning boat."

When they reached the deck, she waved her free hand through the heavy smoke. Eva shadowed them both, staying close so she wouldn't lose them in the haze. Marcus's face appeared nearby, popping in front of them from a cloud that covered the rest of his body. Their eyes met for a brief moment, then he lowered his gaze to her entourage. He nodded at her and motioned crew members toward the location of a small boat. Only those who worked the ship at night would be able to make their way to it.

"Load the dinghy," she verbalized. "We can escape through the smoke."

Overhearing the brief discussion, Eva ran ahead to help. Everyone met around the dinghy and immediately boarded the lightweight craft. Some clever crew members continued to toss dynamite at the invaders. The effect proved a distraction. Susan handed Freddy to Eva, who was already in the dinghy. Then she jumped in the boat as Marcus lowered it into the water. With several members of the crew, he steadied the boat with the ropes and pulleys. Other mates prepared to row as soon as the boat touched the water's surface. Another crew mate threw explosives overhead for cover.

Several yards away from the frigate, Susan spied the two company ships that had attacked them. The black skull and bones flags danced above leaping flames. Marcus glanced at the wreckage for only a moment. Wiping his brow, he shook his head and took an oar in hand.

"I see that you managed to get off some shots before we left," Susan observed.

Marcus shuddered and began rowing. He didn't respond, letting his actions speak instead.

"Close your eyes, Freddy," Susan whispered. "It is not a sight I want you to remember."

Freddy tightly covered his eyes with his little hands. Eva looked away, securely clutching the goods around her. Several of the crew members took a deep breath and focused on the outline of the captain's ship in the distance. Being unimpressive in comparison to the frigate, the corporate raiders had left it untouched. In addition, the ship had maintained a respectful distance to thwart attackers.

"Keep rowing," Marcus ordered in a hushed voice. "We aren't out of the haze yet. The captain won't see us until we are only a few yards away. Then we sail away before any other survivors arrive."

"I don't think they'll approach the boat," a mate commented. "The captain has his cannons ready to fire."

Freddy opened his eyes and glanced at Marcus. Both gaped at the mouths of the cannons emerging clearly through the lingering vapor. Marcus took off his familiar striped shirt, mounted it on a musket, and waved it high in the air like a flag.

"Hey, that's my favorite shirt," jested another crew member.

"You look good in blue," another mate joked.

Marcus ignored the rapport in the boat, and twirled the flag in the air with even more fury. "I don't want to get shot."

"Freddy close your eyes again," Susan said.

"We're not going to get shot," Freddy told them as he lowered his arms. "The captain knows that shirt."

Marcus relaxed and looked down at Freddy.

"You're just in time for breakfast," a voice announced from above the fog. "Here, catch these ropes and we'll reel you in."

Dropping their oars, the men quickly attached the ropes to the dinghy. Marcus removed the shirt from the gun, and redressed. When all the lines were secured, the small craft was lifted out of the water. One by one, people slowly made their way on deck.

"Lose a frigate, gain a son," the captain said as he lifted Freddy into the air and into his arms.

"We sunk two ships," Freddy told him face to face.

Marcus jumped onto the wooden planks and stood beside the captain. Brushing his hair from his forehead, he mentioned, "We released three other dinghies loaded with the ship's stores. They should be adrift in the water somewhere."

He scanned the fog and smoke for unmanned boats. Then stepped back for a better view. A member of the captain's crew joined him and raised his spotting scope.

"The crew will find them. Go grab something to eat before it's gone," the captain advised. Then he put a free arm around Susan and hugged her gently. Placing Freddy back on the ground, he nodded at Eva.

Eva blushed slightly at the deliberate attention. Meanwhile, Freddy ran off chasing Marcus into the dining hall. Susan backed away.

"I have a son almost as old as Freddy. His mother died during his birth," he told Eva in a soft voice.

Hearing his words for Eva, Susan walked away into the mists. She leaned against a rail and scouted the water for intruders. Taking off the sunstone necklace, she put it away momentarily in a pocket. There were no answers to be found in the sunstone or gray smoke.

A member of Marcus's crew came near her. "Looks like you no longer need the necklace to walk. You're recovering from the time wrinkle in India."

Susan kept her focus on the thin outline of the water's surface. Taking a deep breath in relief, she blinked and smiled in return. Then she shrugged her shoulders before turning to face him.

"Look, there at the dawn breaking through," he said, pointing a finger at an opposite direction. "It's two of our dinghies."

Susan left him as he roused the interest of the captain's crew. Grabbing ropes, men hurried toward the area in excitement. She got out of their way and took a detour route to visit Matilda before breakfast. The cow offered a low moo when she entered the stall. Sitting down on a hay bale, she rubbed the cow's fine, soft fur. Within a few minutes, small footsteps became audible in the room.

Munching on a roll, Freddy entered the room. "Here, I brought you and Matilda a snack."

Susan took the muffin from his extended hand, and thanked him. Meanwhile, he savored his piece of bread like he was playing a harmonica. His two small hands held the food near his mouth as he playfully danced on both feet.

"Do you think the captain likes Eva?" he asked, moving closer to Susan.

"Oh, he loved Eva when they carried her aboard from India," she said. "I think that Eva likes the captain now. John Andre became too wordy."

"How do you know these things?" Freddy asked her.

"I had four older brothers," Susan answered. "They were always talking about women between philosophies and prophesies."

Their conversation was interrupted by the sudden appearance of Eva in the doorway. Though she had arrived undetected by the others, Eva gave no indication that she had overheard them. Her eyes searched the room for the reason for the gathering. Susan took another bite from her roll, and left without any explanation. Freddy finished his meal before giving Eva a parting glance. Then he left her alone in the stall with Matilda.

Chapter Eight

Shielding and

Rebuilding the world

Heart by heart

Reference Tune: *Nothing's Gonna Stop Us Now*

----Jefferson Starship

REACHING THE DECK, Susan met the captain waiting for her at the top of the stairs.

"There's more food in the kitchen. Eva made some chai. Bring your cup to the helm," he said. "We need to discuss our next course of action. The wind is picking up." Then he waved his hand in the direction of the wrecked ships, "The smoke will clear soon."

Marcus, who had been standing nearby, piped, "We need to decide whether to run or salvage."

Susan brightened at the options Marcus presented. She skipped to the kitchen and enjoyed a hearty breakfast. Freddy had already beaten her to the table for seconds.

"The danger appears to be over," a crew member remarked. "No alert has been sounded since we boarded. There is only one more dinghy left to find."

"It is worth the risk to stay and retrieve it," Susan commented. Then she left the table and carried her cup of warm chai with her.

At the wheel of the ship, she stood near the captain with her mug. Susan pulled the sunstone necklace from her pocket and examined it closely. The reflections of the dawn streaking through the smoky air shone brightly in the stone. The captain lowered his spotting scope before addressing her. He kept his eye steady on the gray area ahead.

"We sent a boat of scouts to investigate," he told Susan. "We have seen no signs of life since the fire subsided."

Susan looked down at the sunstone and held it in her hand. A strong wind blew across the deck. She looked around the boat for the effects. Everything that was not tied down rattled a few feet across the deck. The watery surface of her drink moved as if she had breathed over it.

"There's our frigate." Marcus turned around and pointed assuredly to Susan. The captain raised his spotting scope to check. "A few minor repairs will make her seaworthy again."

"Susan, do you think we are still experiencing time aberrations?' the captain asked. He dropped his scope as if it was mere toy. He shot a look at Susan and nodded at the necklace. "We must be unraveling ourselves from the disaster in India."

Susan gazed at the frigate on the water, then she studied the necklace again. Smiling for the first time since the battle, she told him, "Yes, we are walking away unscathed. There is no sign of the corporate pirates."

"Only a few rafts with supplies," Marcus said, waving his arms with excitement. His signal caught the attention of the ship's crew and they gathered around him. He exclaimed, "Look, there's our last dinghy! The boat never went far from the ship."

"Hooray!" a mate shouted, scrambling to retrieve the craft. "We have reserves."

"Rest up," the captain ordered. "The scouts will return soon with a full report. Our crew will stand watch. We'll alert you if we get attacked by unseen forces."

The crew from the frigate dispersed, finding their former quarters on the ship. Susan, Freddy, and Eva returned to the hammocks in the hold. Several hours later, Susan awoke. Freddy snored softly in his bed near them.

Eva seemed fully conscious in the semidarkness. She called to Susan, "What happens next?"

Susan stirred in the hammock. Sensing that Eva was worried about her future, she replied, "We split up to avoid further detection. Marcus and the frigate go to Nova Scotia to evade the slave ships. Meanwhile, we go with the captain to Jamaica. We'll meet up in Boston Harbor. It is close to the co-op in Concord, Massachusetts."

"Huh?" Eva questioned. She swung back and forth in her hammock, reflecting on the possibilities.

Susan slid out of her hammock and placed her feet solidly on the ground. Donning an altered pair of Marcus's pants instead of her skirt, she dressed and told Eva, "I need to discuss this with the captain first." Then she moved closer to Eva until they were face to face. Stopping the rhythmic motion of the hemp mat, she winked at Eva. "I'll put in a good word for you with the captain, but I don't think that will be necessary."

Eva smiled, folding her hands over her chest. Susan left Eva in her moment of contemplation. As she ascended the stairs, a wee voice interrupted the silence.

"I'm coming too," Freddy said. He raised his head from the pillow on the woven mesh. Someone had thoughtfully roped a third hammock in the area for his slumber.

Susan looked in his direction but did not respond. He hopped out of bed to follow her. Eva moved from her hammock and looked for a spare pair of pants that would match her adult figure.

"Everything appears as it seems," the captain mentioned to Susan when she joined him at the helm.

"I am thinking that we should split up," Susan told him. "Eva and Freddy will be less noticeable if we reach America by way of Jamaica. The frigate won't be recognized in Nova Scotia. We can meet in Boston."

"Sounds good," the captain commented. His shoulders relaxed as if a huge weight had been lifted. He surmised, "It is all about the big picture. We are just a little boat in a big ocean."

"Yes, but we are thriving in the big ocean. The bigger ships are not."

"They are missing the big picture," he observed.

"They missed the boat," she said.

The captain sighed. Looking down at the lines etched in the wood planks beneath his feet, "We are building a new world in America."

****

Two months later, the captain's ship made its way through time to Jamaica. After docking in the harbor, the captain went ashore to buy more supplies. For various reasons, he preferred not to sell their wares in Jamaica. Eva remained behind to guard the ship with half the crew, which consisted of four other crew members.

"It is still the same old slave trade. The front company only switched nationalities from Spain to England," the captain whispered to Susan as she and Freddy prepared to go shopping in town. He nodded to Freddy. "Your royal stamp will pull some strings here. Just avoid the bazaars operated by the religious orders."

"Why?" Freddy asked.

"The papacy, France, and Spain have recently expelled the holy secret police. These police dress like clergy, but they are controlled ultimately by the same puppet strings that killed your cousin in India," the captain told him. "Please return by sundown. I don't want to stay long in these harbors."

Without any further explanation, the captain hurried into town. The rest of the crew went along to provide assistance and shop. Eva ran toward Susan before she left with Freddy.

"Find me a pretty, new dress," Eva requested. "My husband gave me some money before he died. I can pay for the dress."

Susan surveyed the bustling shops on the other side of the harbor. She nervously replied, "We will look, but no promises."

Freddy glanced up at Susan, "Let's get off this ship before we miss our chance."

Susan and Freddy ran to town, slowing down when they met the hawkers on the outskirts. Quickly bypassing the noisy merchants, they toured a few shops. Freddy bought a pair of pants and a new shirt. He had rapidly outgrown the clothes he wore in India.

"No more hand-me-downs from the crew," he commented as he showed his royal stamp to buy the items. He shelled out some coins from his pocket, and placed them in the hands of the awed shopkeeper. "You and Eva have been beating me to them."

"Let's get out of here," Susan said. "The merchant is excited about the royal appearance. He is summoning British officials."

"I agree," Freddy stated, grabbing his purchase from the store. "I am not ready for any ceremony involving the Duke of York."

The Duke of York sufficed as Freddy's official title as the second son of the English king. Susan held onto Freddy's shirt sleeve and led him through the crowd gathering in the shop. When they were outside the throng, she pointed to a dress shop across the street.

"No," Freddy said. "This one over here. Eva should have a dress like the one that my sisters wear. Let's return to the ship with a princess dress."

"You are right," Susan announced as she followed after the young prince scurrying over to the women's dress shop.

Entering the store simultaneously, they stopped to catch their breath and gaze at the beautiful display of feminine formal attire. Freddy turned his head in several different directions, before he pointed at a gown in the far corner. Susan's eyes grew wide when she spotted the dress that had caught his eye.

"That one," he said.

"Oh, Freddy. It's beautiful," Susan gasped. "The dress will look wonderful on Eva."

Before she could utter another word, Freddy approached the merchant with his royal stamp. He told her, "I have a woman friend who is interested in this dress. She is on board the ship over there in the harbor. I would like to bring it to her, and my friend can return with full payment."

After checking the royal stamp, the shopkeeper eagerly responded to Freddy's request and packaged the gown in a matter of seconds. Freddy slung the bundle over his shoulder before racing Eva to the ship. Breathlessly, the children presented the parcel to Eva. Dodging inside the captain's vacant quarters, she tugged and removed the ties around the package. The unwrapped gown flew high in the air as Eva lifted it from the parchment. She held it against her body to determine its fit. With a decisive nod, she retrieved some coins for Susan.

"Thank you, so much," she said to them. Handing Susan the payment, "Please, give this to the seller."

Susan collected the coins from Eva and skipped across the deck of the ship. She hopped onto the dock and ran back to pay the merchant. With a broad smile, the merchant accepted the payment from Susan who left the shop almost as quickly as she entered. On the way back, she spied a silver hair clasp on a hawker's bargaining table. Depositing a few coins in the palms of the dark-skinned man, she tucked the purchase away in her skirt pocket.

When she arrived on the ship, the captain gave the order for departure. The crew had already started freeing the ship from the dock. Susan went below to check on Matilda. She found Freddy milking the cow. Extending her open hand, Susan showed him the silver hair clasp.

"That's nice," he said, glancing over his shoulder.

Susan pocketed the clasp again, and braced as the ship moved away from town.

"Where are we going now?" Susan asked.

"The crew wants to beach on a deserted island for the afternoon," he told her. "Eva waits for the captain in his quarters."

Chapter Nine

There are different kinds of fire
All must be faced
Never turn your back on a cliff
Never turn your back on a fire

Reference Tune: *Face The Fire*
----Dan Fogelberg

AFTER THE SHIP distanced itself from the town's onlookers, the captain returned to his quarters to consult his map. Eva stood in the doorway several steps from the threshold. She wore the long purple, silk gown with the low cut bodice.

"Eva," the captain murmured. "You look very nice." Then he added under his breath. "As usual."

He stood still with the door still hanging ajar. Eva rushed closer, pausing inches away from his face. One hand of the captain's deftly closed the door behind him and locked it. The other hand reached for Eva's cheek to brush away a strand of hair. Moving closer, he kissed the bared skin as he grasped the dark hair and fingered the soft, shiny fibers. His trembling lips reached for her mouth, and he sought her. Eva dropped her shoulders, relaxing under his caress. He had sailed through many storms and navigated the sea of consciousness with a deliberate decisive air. No words were necessary to convey his sense of elation.

Removing Eva's garment over one shoulder, he palmed her exposed shoulder through the heat of his touch. Eva swooned, captivated by his embrace. Her head fell against his chest as if she had passed out. He lifted her into his arms, carrying her limp body to his bed. The world swirled around them and nothing else mattered for the moment. All the maps and compasses in the room were inside him now. She had become his destination, his point of departure from the past into the future.

Placing Eva on the down mattress before him, he heard her sigh as she closed her eyes. He swiftly unlaced the bodice and exposed her full, rounded breasts. With a gentle tug, he removed the rest of the violet gown from her light brown skin. His eyes feasted on the released female figure before him as he removed his pea coat and began unbuttoning his shirt. Eva's eyes flickered when the tufts of hair surfaced on his chest. Her hands groped for the buttons on his trousers. When she found him, she brought his firmed resolve to her. Together they sailed in the wild sea of consciousness, finding a place where they both could be free to pursue love. Pursuing more than the passion of their desire, they reveled in the mystery which had bought them to this voyage. They were fueled by the spiritual mission to bring their rebirth lives to America, the next stopping point on the mutual horizon.

"I love you, Eva," the captain whispered as he rode her waves through rocky terrain.

She lifted him above the clouds into a celestial realm filled with the brightness of a star-studded sky. Without needing the sun to guide them during the fervor, they learned how to find their way through the night.

"I love you," she repeated, finding his tender lips. She sought him inside her, and he complied with all the seasoned elegance befitting a man of the sea.

Together they drifted toward the unknown, a future limited by the shackles of spells they could not overcome. Paradise for them was just a fleeting moment in the sun. Like eagles, they flew high above the turbulent waves of outcomes they could not control. They spent their lives in the moment. This is what they had understood from the first moment they beheld each other, the time a crew mate had carried Eva on board like a pirated treasure chest.

They awoke from their somnolence to the sound of splashing water. Entangling himself from the rapturous embrace with Eva, he shook his head to regain full consciousness. Eva stirred beside him and opened her eyes. Her black pupils stared wide at the change in scenery. The surroundings spoke of a transformation that she had earlier conceived.

Still naked from the encounter with the woman on his bed, he rose and peered through the small porthole above him. His ship no longer moved. The crew had moored it in a lagoon. In his view of the changing world outside his quarters, he watched several naked bodies dive off a dinghy in the distance.

"Our crew has decided to go skinny-dipping around the island," he told Eva, who remained lying on the bed.

"I want to look," she said, rising from the bed. She looked through the peephole in time to watch Susan and Freddy jump into the water. She observed, "They are having fun."

"Don't leave me," the captain pled in a low voice. Holding her in his arms, he kissed the nape of her neck.

Eva turned around and gazed into his eyes. Putting her index finger over his lips, she informed him in a tone that suited her pragmatic disposition, "I won't. I'm moving in."

Choosing the casual skirt that she wore when entering his quarters, she began dressing in front of him. Her determined, no-nonsense manner contrasted with the subtle seduction of their previous encounter. The captain backed away from her and chuckled. Stepping into his pants, he said, "I'll help you bring your things from the hold."

By the time the crew arrived from sunbathing, Eva had settled into the captain's quarters. No one expressed surprise at the new sleeping arrangements. Following suit, Freddy established a suite near Matilda's stall. Always looking for a party, Freddy waylaid anyone wishing to confer with the cow. He became the cow's ambassador, creating milk schedules while entertaining gossip about her other life as his pet. Susan remained in the hold alone and welcomed the occasion to collect her thoughts as the ship neared America. She sensed that the solitude would be short-lived once her mission as an Eagle became more operational.

When the ship anchored off the Florida coast, the captain and Eva rowed into the harbor. Eva wore her beautiful gown and the couple enjoyed cultivating the port's nightlife scene. Susan remained on board with half the crew, while Freddy and the others took a different dinghy. While the couple attended to business during formal dinners, the crew bartered in local pubs. It proved a productive arrangement for the ship's inhabitants. They stayed an extra day, making it two nights instead of the usual one.

Early the following morning, the captain brought down some wood planks and carpentry tools into the hold. Susan, who had been lingering in her hammock contemplating world voyages, raised her head in greeting. Setting the wood aside, he waved at her and announced, "You have the quarter's upstairs. Eva needs more space in our relationship."

Susan left her hammock and examined the pieces that he had hauled with him. "It looks like you are building a master suite in the hold."

"Yes, I am," he said with a firm nod. "It will be big enough for two. You get the bed upstairs. I think that we will be requiring more of your services in the days ahead. I should have this place finished by the time we reach North Carolina."

Susan gathered her things on condition that the captain would teach her building techniques. She promised to return for the first lesson after she tossed her belongings in her new quarters. Handing her a hammer when she joined him, the captain explained his design. Susan wielded the hammer over well-placed nails while she considered the latest turn of events. For a brief moment, she studied the sunstone necklace in her palm. The elixir of love had altered their course. A sense of randomness and freedom had been distilled in their destinies. Nobody knew where this would take them.

Chapter Ten

Make way

There's a lot at stake

Reference Tune: *Truckin'*

----Bread

SUSAN DOWNPLAYED THE competition between her and the captain by making his quarters available to everyone. During the day, Freddy often came and played in the room. He visited with Susan while she enjoyed being off duty, leaving for his suite at night to sleep in his own quarters. Carefully arranged bales of hay defined his space next to Matilda. He changed the position of the stacks to suit his fancy. Sometimes he made tunnels and slept in a burrow. Other times, he made a bed high above the wood floor. On occasion, he recreated a fort similar to the one they had used earlier. Matilda responded well to his presence, and her milk production remained constant.

At night, Susan shared the room with those who watched the ship with her. The ship's crew became her brothers and she traded shifts with two other crew mates. One of them usually napped in one of the bunks while she worked on deck. The proximity of the room to the helm and shift rotations helped Susan keep her pulse on the ship's voyage.

The captain converted her former place in the hold into a cozy suite. No one ventured into the area unless invited, which seldom happened. Tucked away in a private corner of the ship, the assortment of well-placed curtains and planks protected Eva and the captain from wanderers. It provided another wall of defense from intruders getting past the deck hands. After leaving Florida, the captain required less public exposure and accessibility. No one questioned his reasons; they only grasped the need for action. Though the crew and ship needed protection, they feared appearing disloyal in the eyes of the captain if they consulted Susan.

When they docked in North Carolina, one of the town's leading citizens asked the captain over to his plantation for dinner. He greeted the ship when it arrived in the harbor and pressed the people on board for an immediate response. The captain accepted with one eyebrow raised. After the man disappeared down the wharf, the captain and Eva went into town as a couple to conduct business. A third of the crew went onshore to assist with the trades. They returned late in the afternoon, and the rest of the crew toured the city. Susan and Freddy stayed on the ship because they preferred checking out a city in the dawning hours, rather than risk being witness to its bawdy nightlife.

Using the mirror in Susan's new quarters, Eva applied some make-up to her face. She wore the purple dress that she had bought in Jamaica. Both Susan and Freddy watched her change her appearance for the formal occasion.

"The captain doesn't seem too excited about the party," Susan remarked. "He thinks that he has one up on everyone around."

"How do you know?" Freddy asked.

"He raised an eye brow," Susan replied. "He only does that on suspicion."

Eva lowered her hand with the eyeliner and sighed. She stared at her reflection in the mirror. Susan peered in the mirror to spy on Eva's reaction. Unshed tears flooded Eva's eyes, and Susan shrugged at Freddy.

The captain's knock on the door interrupted them. Holding out his arm for Eva, the man took her away from them. Susan and Freddy followed behind, stopping short of the rail near their exit. The children saw the couple leave the ship for a horse drawn carriage at the end of the wharf. Night descended on them shortly, and Freddy hurried below deck to sleep. After a light meal, Susan rested before her shift.

When she awoke for her rotation on night watch, Susan approached the helm and asked the mate, "Have Eva and the captain returned yet?"

"No, everyone wonders about the captain these days," the mate answered. "Those who are awake are getting worried. We expected them back by now."

"Let's get an extra hand on deck," Susan suggested. "I want to go check on them. I suspect trouble."

"Ay ay," the mate replied. Then he gave her directions to the party.

Susan dressed in a pair of pants that Marcus had given her. With her brown hair tied behind in the silver clasp, she could have been easily mistaken for a male deck hand from a distant view. Leaping off the boat, Susan landing on the wharf. She ran in the shadows to a house at the other end of town.

"Who are you?" a woman questioned her. Emerging from the bush where she had been throwing up, she teetered from side to side. She was dressed in a long gown with hooped skirt. She was unable to move with any great speed in her attire.

Surprised by the woman stepping out of the darkness, Susan fled for refuge behind some bushes fifty yards away. She took advantage of her debilitated pursuer wearing such awkward dress. Susan flattened her body on the ground and crawled into a hiding position where she could see the woman. Appearing flustered, the woman took a few steps in Susan's direction and stopped abruptly.

"I know you're out there," she said, slurring her words. "You've come for the people John Paul locked in the basement."

Susan rose from underneath the foliage. "Who is John Paul?"

"You don't know John Paul Jones?" the woman questioned. "He recognized the captain from Cape Horn." The woman quieted briefly. "How come you have a girl's voice and boy's clothes?"

"It's a long story," Susan quipped, maintaining a safe distance from the inebriated mistress.

"Wanna borrow one of my dresses?" the woman asked. "John Paul is fond of young women who still have figures like boys. I'm not having any luck tonight. Let's have some fun."

"How angry are you at John Paul?" Susan asked.

"Enough to dress you up and help you get the keys to the basement from John Paul," the woman told her. "Just don't sleep with him. He's mine."

"Not a problem," Susan said as she walked toward the woman. "It's a deal."

Moments later, Susan unlocked the door to the basement. Clad in a long pink ballroom gown, she ushered the captain and Eva out of the house. Although they momentarily stared wide-eyed at Susan's appearance, they wordlessly dashed for the nearby forest. Together they made their way back to the boat while a crescent moon broke through the heavy black fog enveloping them. The captain stopped briefly and pointed to the emergence of a stag calmly gazing in a clearing before them. When the animal detected their arrival, he leapt in the air and skirted the path leading directly to their ship.

Eva and Susan raced to the ship to change their clothes. The captain signaled for all hands to be on deck before tugging at the ropes on the wharf. The night shift began raising the anchor and maneuvering the lines he fed them. Thickening ebony haze concealed their immediate departure from North Carolina.

Matilda had already roused Freddy from his slumber, and he met the frantic crew members as they ran upstairs. Instead of joining the shipmates around the helm, he stood in front of the door to Susan's room. Leaning against the wood frame, he crossed his arms as he waited. Surveying her formal attire from top to bottom, he observed, "You're a quick learner." He uncrossed his arms before crossing the threshold. "I want to know all the details."

She breezed past him to her quarters, allowing him to follow her inside. She pulled her blouse from the bust of the bodice. Lifting the dress over her head, she revealed her trousers underneath the hem. Freddy closed the door behind them, and she spoke while changing. "It's only an act. I seized the role like a pirate's treasure. I wanted a nice dress." Then she glanced at Freddy and explained, "Unfortunately, the prize comes with risks."

"What do you mean?" he asked, straightening up. "It looks like to me like you rescued Eva and the captain."

"True," Susan said as she buttoned her blouse. "That proved risky, too." Stooping over her shoes to fasten them, she added, "In fact, our enemies are coming after us."

"What? When? Where? And Whom?" Freddy questioned her. He crossed his arms in frustration at her response. "Don't get poetic or philosophical with me. I am not John Andre."

"True," Susan answered, applying final touches to her transformation from seducer to deck hand. Then she eyed him carefully before saying, "You're one to talk."

She lifted the dress from the ground and ceremoniously hung it on a peg like it was a trophy. Then she stopped to regain her balance as her legs wobbled with the ship's abrupt movement. Both she and Freddy stood back to admire the latest acquisition.

A knock on the door interrupted their discourse. The captain's head peered in the room. Looking at Susan, he firmly told her, "Relax for a moment. Everything is under control. Nobody will be able to find us in this fog. It is like we found a hidden hole in the ground."

The captain left as quickly as he entered, shutting the door securely. Susan sat down on the bed and folded her legs. Freddy climbed to the upper bunk across from her and nested.

Looking up at his young eager face, she began, "The major slaveholder in the area invited the captain and Eva over. During dinner, he locked them in the basement. He intended for his business partner to extort the captain." Susan gulped and stared wistfully into space. "It gets complicated quickly. There is no easy explanation."

"Try me," Freddy retorted.

Susan continued, "I ran into the mistress of the extortionist while investigating the premises. I took advantage of the fact that she was drunk and wearing a hooped skirt. She told me, 'Those who can't handle the cats, play with the kittens.' So she gave me this dress and I got to play like a kitten. Only I discovered that I really had the manners of a cat, and easily extracted the keys to the basement from her former lover. He never touched me. Instead, her lover fell for the man who threw the party. I understand that Mr. Jones of North Carolina intends to set up Mrs. Jones with a fleet of ships."

Freddy softly whistled. "It must have been some party!"

"True," Susan repeated. Tossing her head from side to side as if attempting to balance the events of the evening, she reflected, "I can understand why I found Mr. Paul's mistress throwing up in the bushes. It was more than just the name change. I think she wanted her own company of ships."

"Matilda is going to have to sleep by herself tonight," Freddy commented. "I'm staying here with all the action."

Another knock at the door interrupted the conversation. A low voice became audible from behind the door. "All hands on deck. We have visitors." Opening the door slightly, several wide-eyed crew members murmured, "The captain sought help from the divine spirits of Diana and Cerridwen. A stag from the forest appeared on the dock as we left. It was their stag."

"What?" Freddy and Susan echoed. "Nobody ever told us about the captain's connection to the Greek and Welsh goddesses."

"It happens from time to time," a crew member whispered as they led the children to the ship's wheel. "The divine connection and your sunstone necklace opened a portal to the MidEarth. A hauflin and Blue fairy came aboard."

"What's a hauflin?" Freddy asked softly.

"They are the guardians of the MidEarth. That is another long story. The hauflins are half human and half earth spirit, whereas a fairy is fully an earth spirit," Susan explained.

All of those on the ship focused their attention on the figures standing opposite the ship's wheel. The hauflin stood about three feet high. He was barefoot with tufts of fur on his feet. Wearing a checkered vest and corduroy pants, he resembled an English country gentleman. His wrinkled forehead and graying temples distinguished his grave, serious demeanor. Occasionally, he directed his pipe at various crew mates for emphasis in the short discussion brewing on the deck. The Blue fairy stood a few feet behind him. She had assumed a human form for this meeting and beamed at the gathering crowd.

Serving as ambassador for the Fairy Queen, who had ruled since the days of ancient Egypt, the hauflin announced, "Hi, folks." Shaking the hands of those close, he continued, "Nice to meet you. You can call me Bilbo."

The crew hushed with his introduction.

"The Queen of the Fairies has an important message," Bilbo continued. Stepping aside, he took a few puffs of his pipe, and offered the floor to the Blue fairy with a bow.

In a warm voice, she addressed the ship's occupants and described the horrors of the present painful conditions. "The scales of justice are no longer balanced in the human world. The escalating slave trade persecutes the human spirit. Sauron, the evil sorcerer, has returned to entrap the human spirit. Those who pirate human lives practice black magic."

After a moment of silence, the Blue fairy told them, "We forge a new contract with the human world. Many will die in battle. Their souls will require transport for survival underneath the harsh conditions. The Blue fairies are taking over the soul transport network. We will carry only those warriors who die freeing the earth from Sauron's grasp. The rest will perish."

When she finished, the Blue fairy backed away from the group. Bilbo jumped between her and the ship's crew. Everyone remained still; some looked at each other and nodded their support of the new contract.

The captain summarized the assembly's reaction. Speaking for the crew, he said, "Thanks for your help. We need all we can get." Then he waved them away, so that the rest could get back to sleep.

Appearing slightly bewildered by the lack of resistance, Bilbo waved his arms in the air briefly for crowd control. When everyone walked away without a fight, he apologized, "Gosh, if we had known how bad things had gone, we would have thought of something sooner. Thanks for your enthusiastic support."

His last phrase fell ironically flat on the dispersing crowd. The expression on their faces was one of blissful relief. The captain waved good-bye to the visitors from the MidEarth. He explained, "We need to have fun together more often. This crisis management mode gets a little stale. Don't get us wrong. It's been a rough night and the passengers are weary."

The couple left, fading into the vapor of the black fog. When they had completely vanished, Susan and Freddy returned to the captain's quarters. They settled in their beds and awoke refreshed the next morning. While he continued sleeping in the bunk, Susan dressed and went on deck. Only a few sailors were present in the crisp early morning air. A light sea breeze tugged at the masts, and created minor ripples in the white sheets overhead. With

North Carolina miles behind them, the frothy wake emphasized the distance between them. Visibility had returned accentuating the crystal blue skies laced with billowing clouds. On the near horizon rose a series of small islands with inviting sandy beaches.

Eva stood next to the captain at the helm. Raising her head slightly, there was a sense of yearning in her eyes. Nodding in the direction of the island, the rest of her body remained motionless as she suggested, "Let's stop. I want to go for a swim."

The captain jumped a little in his stance. Looking at her near his shoulder, he told her, "Great idea. Take Freddy and two of the crew. The rest of us will regroup after last night's events." Then he turned in Susan's direction, "Stay on board. We need to talk."

Susan walked away from the competition for control at the ship's wheel. She waited in the distance, leaning over the rail to gaze at the waters below. Both hands clasped casually over the edge, and she straightened to assume a more reflective posture. The motion signaled a change from the depths of her soul. Usually, she studied external reflections in the sunstone, sky, or sea waves. This time the answers seemed to stir from within. She had found an alternate route, which proposed a win-win situation.

When the ship anchored in the bay, the captain handed Susan a cup of tea before beckoning her to a desk at the far end of the ship. The beached crew threw off their clothes and played in the small, unfurling waves. The rest of the crew caught up on meals and sleep. The captain rested in a chair near the desk, after offering Susan a place to sit.

Staring at Susan directly, he began, "There is something wrong with our visitors from the MidEarth. They seem jaded."

Susan commented, "I agree. Some changes need to be made. I can go to MidEarth and check things out."

The captain glanced at Eva frolicking in the surf, and studied his hands on the table. "I have something I should tell you. You don't know much of my story. No one does."

Susan shifted in her chair uncomfortably. "I don't know your name."

"Captain Robert Drake," he said. "My father was kidnapped by the decorated pirate Francis Drake and left on an isolated island to be tortured by Spanish Inquisitors. The inhuman Spanish marooned him. His father, Thomas Drake took issue with the pirating of the family crest."

"I understand that Queen Elizabeth's Drake became a reptilian dragon rather than a family man," Susan said, folding her hands on the table. "My brothers talked about the groups responsible for legalizing human trafficking. Lord Russell, the man who botched Henry VIII's mission with the pope, stole the name along with the Tavistock property. It had belonged to a monk by the name of Drake. When the monk bequeathed the land to his relations, the land went to the Russells and the name went to a newborn of one of their slaves."

"They turned the issue into another holy war," Captain Robert Drake said. "They assumed that there is safety in numbers and converted those they captured for slavery."

"Drake is from the Welsh name for dragon," Susan observed. "It is the same as John Paul stealing the name Jones for business purposes with the man who did away with the Jones in North Carolina."

"Henry II took a spiritual wizard warrior with him to England. They called him Drex, which is a Welsh term for dragon. We come from a family of Dragon flyers descended from King Arthur's knights."

"Yes, I heard about the Green Dragon Tavern as a base for planetary freedom," Susan remarked. "The man in England told Marcus and I about it."

"There's more to it," the captain reflected. "Sauron and his dark cardinal must have infested the MidEarth with their nonsense. Sauron always assumes the name Germain when he is in human form. He is a mortal of vampire proportions. A Germain entered the court of King Arthur and destroyed it from within. I suspect that the Saint Germaine haunting the French parlors is the same entity as the Germain serving England as secretary of state. This means that the fate of the thirteen colonies rests with him, not King George III." Taking a deep breath, he edged closer to Susan as if confiding. He told her, "If he destroys America, then he destroys the MidEarth. They are after the soul of earth."

Susan leaned back in her chair and thought about the implications of his words. She sighed. "We need more than a new contract. It is time we escort our own souls across. The MidEarth must come out and help fight the fight."

"Only Bilbo and Fodor remain in the MidEarth," Captain Drake observed. "They can handle it, while souls go back and forth."

"Their knowledge base makes them useful as assistants," Susan said. "I can access the MidEarth from the ship's rail."

"It is time to intervene before it is too late," the captain announced.

Susan arose, "I'll go talk to the Blue fairy. She can be birthed in a human form at a future date."

"There are many details to work out," he said, gathering his things from the table. The captain motioned for members of the crew to put away the table and chairs. People were returning from the beach, and it was time to sail away. Pacing his steps with Susan, he bowed his head before adding,

"Tavistock has now become headquarters for mind control agendas. King George is not the only one going crazy these days."

"History has seen this play out before," Susan remarked. "My brothers speculated that Sauron's minions will push on Mozart."

"Bloodletting and vaccinations are reaching epidemic proportions, while bioterrorism prevails. Although, they are useful occasionally, the procedures are being overdone for assassinations and genocide," the captain remarked. "The academic societies emerging from the dark ages recklessly pursue enlightenment. The Renaissance came and went. Now that the world financiers have succeeded in removing the soul from the body, they are systematically inoculating the demon into the human form. By the next century, the gothic art forms will become horrific."

"It is a madness setting on the planet," Susan observed. "Like Eagles we must fly before they shackle us all."

Susan and the captain concluded their meeting. When Eva returned, the captain accompanied her to their suite in the hold, while Susan travelled through the MidEarth portal. Instead of going to Bilbo's shire, she chose to directly deal with the Blue fairy. The Blue fairy and her kingdom had taken refuge on a lush, tropical island. The island existed fifteen dimensions from the Earth. Susan arrived in a community area where the Blue fairy held court.

"I am happy to see you," the Blue fairy greeted. She smiled at Susan and playfully tossed a coconut at her. Susan grinned and caught the coconut, then she hurled it back at the fairy. The Blue fairy quickly rose to field the coconut. The court adjourned and people scattered while the two played. As they continued throwing the coconut back and forth, the fairy said, "It is about time that the Fairy Kingdom got back into the action."

"Time to play," Susan told her, putting more might in her throws after the fairy drilled the coconut at her. "This may be the only free time on the beach that I get."

"You have rivals on your own ship. It will take us a series of four generations to convert to the human form," the fairy said. "We have to learn how to play the game."

"There's no rush," Susan quipped. She danced around with the coconut before the next throw. "What matters is that you get started. This is the best way to correct the imbalance."

"Have you talked to Bilbo? Does he want to play?" the Blue fairy asked. Then she added, "You are over the loss of your brothers."

"No, I don't want to play with Bilbo. He and Fodor no longer possess the same lightness of spirit required to deal with the havoc on the earth plane," Susan responded as she caught the coconut in midair and ran around with it.

"What are you going to do about them?" the fairy questioned her.

"I'll make them assistants. They become custodians of the MidEarth so that we all have a place to rest between transitions," Susan answered.

"What are you going to do about them?" the Blue fairy repeated.

"Oh, the captain and Eva," Susan observed. "Eva and the captain envy my play, and take what isn't theirs to give. I am not the captain of my fate, in this regard. Nor am I the captain, much less an intimate of Eva."

"No, they are not generous friends," the Blue fairy commented. "Your allegiance is to the honor imbued in the necklace that brought you to me."

"Yes, there is a code in the necklace. My brothers told me about a place called Camelon in Scotland. The necklace represents a time when the MidEarth did not have to hide."

Without a further word, the fairy held on to the coconut. She nodded and smiled at Susan, who faded away once she felt assured of the fairy's participation in the divine scheme.

Back on the boat, she met the captain at the helm. "We got 'em."

"And Bilbo and Fodor?" he asked.

"The fairy will talk to them. Bilbo and Fodor will cooperate. They don't have to make any changes and will be happy to stay in the shire."

Several hours later, while Susan and most of the crew slept, the Blue fairy and Bilbo reappeared on the ship. Standing at the wheeling, he saw a familiar black fog envelop the ship. One of the crew members waved at him. "They're back, Captain."

The Blue fairy shimmered in the dark mist before them. Bilbo sauntered over to the captain and sat down on a nearby crate. He beckoned for the Blue fairy to join him

"One of the humans on your ship can travel through the portal to the MidEarth," the Blue fairy began. She stood beside Bilbo. With chagrin she added, "She beat us at our game."

"How's that?" the captain asked. He gave the newcomers his full attention, and called for a mate to relieve him from his duty at the helm.

The two people from the MidEarth never answered him. Instead Bilbo sighed. He mentioned, "We need to change our image."

"I could have told you that," the captain said. "Start with the younger humans and build up a relationship that provides comfort. Some call it parenting, a practice that only works as long as both parties live for a certain amount of years, which is a rarity these days. If you scare them, then the souls will see you and run when it comes time for transport."

"What do you have in mind?" Bilbo questioned.

The captain placed a gold doubloon in the fairy's hand. Closing her fingers over the Spanish coin, he told her, "Freddy lost his wiggly tooth. Use your powers of inter-dimensional travel and place this coin underneath his pillow tomorrow night. I will tell Freddy that the tooth fairy will bring him money for the teeth he loses while growing up."

"You are clever," Bilbo remarked. "With the admirals in the British navy spouting tales of antichrist, survivalism, and ancestral monkeys, we must take care and avoid being harbingers of doom."

"There's another purpose," the captain stated. "It will counter the occultism in world commerce and link world trade to the MidEarth."

Chapter Eleven

The freedom of

Just travelin' and livin'

Reference Tune: *Me And You And A Dog Named Boo*

----Lobo

WHEN THEY DOCKED in New York Harbor, the captain conferred with Eva and Susan. "There is a meeting for Eagles at dusk. The Dutch division of United India Company has the run of the place, so we must be careful to avoid scrutiny. Stay in the Dutch area, and avoid British soldiers."

The captain, Eva, and Susan left the ship shortly before darkness. They hurried across present day Manhattan to a dilapidated farm house. After two knocks on the wooden door to the shed next to the house, the door opened and the captain quickly ushered the women inside. In the dim light of two candles, ten people sat together and spoke in low, inaudible voices. Two men rose from their chairs and offered seats to the newcomers.

The group quieted as the captain related the events of the previous year in ten minutes. Most people seemed familiar with the turn of events from their own experiences. When he finished, a young farmer stood and addressed the others.

"It is time to consider the location of the new capitol," he said. "I suggest New York City Hall in honor of the landmark case for freedom of the press. It is at 73 Pearl Street."

"Are you referring to the Zenger Trial?" someone asked.

"Yes, the argument for freedom of the press came with the pilgrims," the man answered. "People like Bradford ran presses in Holland before getting permission to settle here."

"The Sons of Liberty, an occult group associated with the controllers of the United India Company have been baiting the British soldiers into war," announced another.

"They are calling themselves Knights of the Golden Circle and have been erecting poles, ancient Druid structures that became the occult symbols of the Roman Empire."

"Yes," a woman nodded. "The maypoles of the Druids were hollow cylinders. The strings of ribbon were actually strings of light emanating from the tubes."

"It's a lost technology." The captain sighed.

"Don't worry. It will come to us, once we have the time to remember," a man reflected. "For now, we must construct our new government. The ancient royal fiefdoms have plans to remove the defunct monarchs and kill the surviving natives. Like our young Duke of York and the pilgrims, many have fled here for refuge. The pilgrims wished to establish the Glastonbury orders on this continent as a new beginning."

"I propose that we meet tomorrow at Fraunces Tavern. The address is 54 Pearl Street," another woman said. "Meanwhile, please review the bill of rights."

The group dispersed quietly after a few minor discussions. After the meeting, a cloaked woman drew the captain aside. Eva and Susan paused for a moment and waited for the captain. After a brief discussion with the woman, the captain rejoined them with a pained expression on his face.

"I have someone for you," she whispered to the three of them. "Follow me. He is in good health and spirits."

The threesome left through a back door and walked with the woman over to the main house. The entrance to the cellar was behind locked doors outside the building. Leaning over the closed opening, the woman rapped softly.

"The boy's father is here," she called softly to those on the other side.

Within moments, a small boy appeared from a grove of trees nearby. He dropped the hand of the teenage babysitter, and raced into the arms of the captain. The man bent over the lad, swooping him into his arms.

"There's another entrance to the cellar at the other end of the property," the woman explained to Eva and Susan. "The captain's older son recently died from the fever. He wants to take his other son to Lexington."

After hearing the news, Eva went over to the captain. The woman seized the opportunity to talk to Susan without being overheard. As Eva fawned over the captain's son, Susan followed the woman to another building on the property.

"There's a child for you also," she mentioned, opening a door to the main house.

Stepping inside the bright candlelit room, Susan received a one month old infant from a young woman about three years older. She held the baby in her arms and stared at its face. The baby remained quiet with half-closed eyes.

"He's very handsome," she said. Then she glanced at the woman who had given her the baby. "I remember your face from the meeting."

"This is General Gage's grandson," she said. "My father fought with General Washington during the French and Indian wars."

An older woman extended her hand to Susan. "I am Margaret Gage. Several families at the Lexington cooperative will help you care for your son. Meanwhile, I will see to it that you arrive safely."

Susan studied the faces of the three women around her. Instead of asking questions, she murmured, "Thank you very much. I will love him with all my heart."

Satisfied with Susan's response, Margaret's eyes misted as the younger woman lightly embraced Susan."My name is Maria Theresa Gage. We will be good friends forever."

Susan returned the baby to its young mother for nursing and then left the room. Leaving through another door, she told them, "Do not mention this to the captain, Eva, and the others. The baby is mine, and I do not want further strife from them. They would sabotage my affection out of jealousy."

Margaret lifted her head with a slight understanding smile. There was a sense of hope across her countenance. She said to Susan, "You have a new family now. Someone to love and take care of. He is a very fortunate young man."

Wiping a tear that had escaped her eye, Susan nodded and hurried outside into the dark. The woman who had led her to the infant hurried over to the captain. Susan followed a few steps behind her, staying in the shadows to compose herself and dry her tears. The light withdrawal served its purpose in downplaying her appearance beside Eva and the captain.

Carrying his exuberant son on one shoulder, the captain quickly left the premises after heartily thanking the woman and handing her a dress procured from a boutique in North Carolina. Eva kept pace with the captain's quick steps back to the ship. Occasionally, she rubbed the child's small leg as he smiled at her from his position above. Having already guessed her relationship with the captain, the young boy immediately accepted Eva as part of his fluid, extended family. Sheer delight showed on his face in the moonlight.

"One more night on the town, then we leave for Boston," the captain whispered as the group made their way back to the boat.

"What's your name?" Eva questioned the little boy.

"Bernard," he answered. "Call me Bernie."

The next evening, Bernie and Freddy created straw bale forts around Matilda's stall while they attended the next Eagles meeting at Fraunces Tavern. A doorman at the establishment clapped the captain on his back, and led them to a concealed room near the wine cellar. One after the other, they descended a ladder into the confines. The raucous noise from the wooden floors above them diminished as they entered the hidden room with a hard dirt floor. Susan looked around the room and recognized some of the faces. Maria Theresa stood at the opposite end with several other young people.

"The Sons of Liberty are meeting in another hall upstairs," the doorman told them. "Take care to avoid them. The Eagles are literally meeting right under their noses."

A cooper in the closed room stepped forward. After hugging the captain, he thrust some furled papers in the gentleman's hands. He said, "Robert, please review this declaration of our independence with your companions."

"What a delight!" the captain responded.

Eva placed some parchment in the cooper's empty hands. She said, "Here are our notes on the proposed bill of rights. Susan can speak for us."

With the notes in hand, the cooper turned around and spoke to the twenty individuals assembled in the room. "Let's get straight to business before either the patriots or Sons of Liberty find us. Open discussion concerning the Bill of Rights. Susan has the floor."

Susan took a deep breath and began. "Besides freedom of the press, we arrived at five tenets. First, there is the right to assemble for religious reasons, education, or pursuit of happiness. Second, we propose a right to pursue nonviolent options. Third, there is a right for safe passage, commerce, or travel with a caveat on the legal definition of commerce. Fourth, human beings have a right to reproductive freedom, which includes the choice of partners. Fifth, the last right guarantees the freedom of all human beings, if I may add 'no ifs, ands, or buts.'"

"Thank you for your description on the notes presented," the cooper rejoined. "Is there further discussion?"

Several other proposals were added to the working document. They included the right to overthrow unlawful governances, and a right for individual self-expression as long as it didn't interfere with anyone else's self-expression. The meeting adjourned after an hour, long before the others left the tavern. The captain, Eva, and Susan raced back to the ship. The crew was waiting for their arrival. The prepared ship left under the cover of darkness for Boston, the captain's final destination for the time-being.

The next morning, Susan met the captain and Eva at the helm. Some of the crew members had remained on deck to help with operation of the ship while the others rested. Freddy and Bernie remained playing below deck.

One of the mates addressed Susan, "Tell us about last night's meeting."

The captain glanced in her direction, then returned his focus to the horizon. "Yes, I'd like your comment on what transpired."

"The meeting gave us a start on the documentation for our new government, which we will declare unlawful."

"On what basis?" a crew member standing next to her asked.

"It is complicated," Susan began. "My brothers said that America would need to be a separate country to avoid being the pawn of those intending to destroy the monarchies of the world. They projected that the opportunity to expand the stable government of the Spice Route would arise on this continent." After wiping a tear that had escaped her eye, she added, "The nation operating the Spice Route existed only in those who worked with the Eagles knighthood. They were convinced that the spiritual body would find a new world." Backing away from the group she said, "There is a Chinese saying about being able to find opportunity in chaos. The havoc surrounding us may provide the fertility for this new terrain."

Then she went to check on Matilda before anyone interrupted her.

Chapter Twelve

There is no honor in those
Who proudly fight to die

Reference Tune: *Indian Reservation*
----Paul Revere and The Raiders

WHEN THE SHIP docked in Boston Harbor, Eva and Susan went shopping in town to gather supplies for life on a farm. The captain stayed on board to negotiate trades and transfer authority of the ship to his mates. They hurried through the streets to avoid being recognized by those who might consider themselves enemies. Near the heart of town, they encountered a group of slaves from Africa. White-skinned slaves from Britain and Native American slaves were gathering around those from Africa. In the absence of their owners they purposely congregated in the most crowded section to avoid being seen talking to other people captured from other countries. Only a few had legitimately sold themselves as indentured servants.

"You there," an African slave hailed Susan. "You are new in town. What are you looking for?"

"Supplies for a farm co-op," Susan answered.

"You must be from that spice boat," another slave commented as he scrutinized Susan's silent companion.

Eva interjected, "Yes, we are from India."

"Great. We can help each other," one African captive said. "We need quality goods for our masters, and you need help in avoiding our masters."

"Why would your masters come after us?" Susan questioned.

"Our masters are British, Spanish, Dutch and colonist. They destroy any spice ships without slaves, because they consider them revolutionaries."

"Looks like the war started without us," Susan mentioned to Eva, before walking away from the crowd.

Eva lingered with the group. Within moments hands were exchanging shovels and pails for spiced goods. The trading lasted only a matter of minutes. Then Eva shouted to Susan, "Let's get out of here."

"I suggest traveling the outskirts of the city and catching the North Road at the far end of town," an African told them. "Tonight."

"Come and visit us again," another African captive said. "Now you know where to find us. We can tell you many things."

Susan smiled. "It's a deal."

Reaching the ship in a short amount of time, they found the captain loading a covered wagon with various sundries. Matilda was already tied to the wagon and both boys petted the cow while the captain packed. The wagon was drawn by two horses, while a third stood nearby waiting for a rider.

"Ever rode a horse, Eva?" the captain asked.

Eva shook her head. "We must leave immediately, and go around the city to find the North Road."

"You and Susan get to take turns learning," he said, lifting Eva onto the spare horse. "In this part of the world, everyone needs a horse. The boys are too young to learn under the circumstances.

They travelled during the warm summer evening, slowly making their way out of Boston in the darkness. Without stopping, they found the North Road at the outskirts of the city. They rested early the next morning and walked around to adjust to the new terrain. The motions of the horses differed from the rolling waves beneath the ship. By the end of the journey, their stance on land and horse became more stable.

****

In August 1769, they reached the farm cooperative located between the towns of Lexington and Concord. Freddy attended a preparatory school a mile away, while Susan and Bernie went to a smaller, single room facility closer to Lexington. Freddy had a stronger British accent than the other two, and could maintain greater anonymity at the isolated campus. Susan only attended school part-time and worked in a shop established by the cooperative. The shop sold farm products and goods provided by the spice trade. When she wasn't studying or serving customers, Susan gardened and milked Matilda. Between chores, she visited her son several houses away, where she lived with a family in the cooperative. Eva shared a cabin with the captain and Bernie, though she stayed in the kitchen most of the time, providing small meals for those wishing to dine. Choosing to hide from customers at the counter, she remained a strong behind-the-scenes presence, and often chatted with the captain as he filled the wood bin and did errands. Depending on the weather or her mood, Eva either cooked inside or outside. The boys did minor chores and learned from the other three members of their group. Sometimes they did homework behind the counter; sometimes they hunted with the captain, and other times they stirred the pots for Eva. The captain traded his carpentry skills for food and supplies. The captain and Susan made new friends in the social network, while Eva developed a social group from those curious enough to venture from the front counter.

A week after Susan arrived in Lexington, a young man knocked on the door of the cabin. The older woman in the family invited him inside and directed him to Susan and the baby. They shared a small room in the back of the house, where Susan could respond to the infant's needs throughout the night.

"A gentleman is here regarding the baby," the woman announced, ushering him toward the cradle.

Susan glanced at the young man's face. He appeared several years older than her. His hair was blonde and very fine.

Before the older woman said another word, he extended his hand to Susan. "I am the father of the child. I have some money for his support."

Susan glanced at the woman, who smiled at him. She told them, "I recognize you from one of the taverns in New York, except that you were meeting the Sons of Liberty."

Wiping a tear that escaped his eye, he bowed his head and handed a coin purse to Susan. He said, "We are not animals. I was setup. The Culpeper spy ring gave me the devil's apple and tortured me. I am here to make amends. Thank you for taking care of the situation. My classmates at Yale told me where I could find the child. They were at the meeting, too."

"I see," Susan said, handing him the child. "He is a good boy."

The older woman nodded. "Yes, he is easily content and doesn't fuss. We enjoy him very much."

A sense of relief flooded the young man's countenance as he fondly held the infant in his arms. He said, "My name is Nathan Hale. What is his?"

"We call him Greg," Susan said, wiping the forehead of the baby with a damp cloth. "He does well with the summer heat."

"My classmates with the Sons of Liberty want to change. We can't fly with the Eagles, but you can call us the Ducks. We are learning to let things roll off our backs like water."

Nathan spent a moment with William and then handed the baby back to Susan. "I'll return in a few days. I want to find a place to stay in town where I can be close. My class load this semester is light, and I want to help care for the baby. There are starting a stem school program at Yale for bridging the gap between occultism and the Spice Route trafficking."

Nathan returned two days later as promised. He invited Susan to his two room house and sometimes she spent the night there with the baby. Occasionally, he left to study at Yale and address business in Boston and New York. Leaving a key to the house with Susan, he encouraged her to spend more time there. Susan used the site for moments when she required more privacy with the child.

The captain brooded over his lost son, there last of his bloodline. Dividing her time between parenting Greg and going to school with Bernie, Susan sidestepped the unpleasant atmosphere surrounding the captain's cabin. Often she would walk with Bernie to school, pick up her assignment, return to check on her baby, and did her schoolwork during lull times at the cooperative store. Several families rotated shifts with her when the baby awoke, so that she could be by him. For the moment, his needs were simple and he seemed to sense that his primary caretaker was always close, even though she worked a quarter mile away. Susan turned in her homework when she returned to take Bernie home.

By the end of September, several schoolchildren became ill and died. Bernie's ambitious father insisted that he remain at school, and the captain occasionally walked him home in the afternoons. Nobody could determine the cause of the epidemic. One day after bringing Bernie home from school, the captain became bedridden with chills and fever. Eva spent mid-October with the captain and cut back her hours at the store. Susan and other members of the cooperative rotated nursing shifts. Other adults in the community became ill also, and could no longer fulfill their tasks. Fortunately, Greg continued to thrive under her care and eased his mother's burden through the joy he brought her.

When Bernie became ill at school, the head instructor sent a messenger to Susan. Susan hurried to bring Bernie home for care. Entering the back room of the school house, she found Bernie lying on a small bed. His breath was shallow and his face ashen. He barely flickered his eyes when Susan knelt beside his bed. Holding the sunstone necklace in her hands, Susan gazed into its reflections. Then she looked out the window of the room. A beam of sunlight emanated from the autumn sky and streaked across the playground in the direction of the well outside. Taking a deep breath, Susan lifted the small child to her. A light rose from inside the crystal and the child awoke fully. He appeared strong enough to walk some of the way home. The teachers stepped aside as Eva and Bernie left the schoolhouse.

Bernie went straight to bed and stayed in the same room as the captain, who was still weak from the illness.

"Go to the Eagles's meeting at the Green Dragon Tavern in Boston," the captain urged Eva and Susan the next morning. "Tell them that there is an epidemic in the area. Take this letter to my friend from New York. He will be at the meeting. We need to send Freddy to his boarding school in New York before he gets sick, too."

Eva sobbed and lingered with Robert Drake. Then she arranged with friends to care for him and his son, while Susan packed and got the horses ready. Together they rode into Boston under the cover of darkness. Within a block of the Green Dragon Tavern, a man redirected them to Boston Commons.

Taking off his hat, he waved to slow them down. "The Sons of Liberty have attacked the meeting place. They live at Boston Commons and bribed the owner into betraying us. We'll meet at our enemies' well. You can refresh your horses there. We know they won't contaminate their own water."

Susan and Eva turned their horses around as shouts and gunfire erupted from inside the tavern. They hurried across town to Boston Commons. Dismounting near the well, they met the rest of the Eagles there.

"It is possible that one of the wells is contaminated in Lexington," a woman explained when Eva told the story of the illnesses. "The British soldiers contaminated wells with yellow fever for the French Indian wars. Now they want everyone to get vaccines, but it only seems to weaken people."

As Eva and the others conversed, a young teen approached Susan. Smiling at her, he said, "You must be the one working on the documents for America's government. I have some more information for you."

Susan blushed under the light of a single lamp. The young man moved closer to her as some of the others backed away. Susan blinked at his forward, direct manner. "Yes, I have some papers."

"I'll come to Lexington next month to check on things. Here, I brought the information with me. Take it with you and look it over," he instructed. "It is a legal copy of the Treaty at Fort Stanwix."

Susan cocked her head from side to side. She didn't respond to the handsome man's offer. Eva ceased chatting and watched the subtle flirtation between them. Susan responded with a question. "What makes Penn's land-grabbing so significant?"

"The treaty makes the royals look greedy," he commented. "In the name of Parliament, the King has bought the land between the Ohio and Tennessee Rivers." Looking at Eva, he said, "It started this way in India, except the natives were not compensated for their loss."

Susan quieted for a moment, while Eva and the others uncomfortably stepped away from the discussion. Susan looked down at the ground. Picking up a shiny stone from the earth, she reflected, "The British soldiers are still contaminating the wells, though the war between the French and Indians is over. This means that British forces intend to start a war with their own colonists. The purpose is to bring more land under the control of the British Empire rather than provide a haven for refugees and religious dissenters."

"French traders convinced their Native American allies to scalp civilians," the young man continued. "The traders accompanied the influx of a religious order that the pope recently threw out of the church."

Susan dropped the stone. Raising her head to study the passing clouds in the dark sky overhead, she said, "There is a bigger world picture. Ultimately the parliament-driven empire and the French outcasts work for the same serpentine guru in India. Murder for corporate greed has become a barbaric ritual."

"Rumor has it that they intend to infuse the black magic into the currency," the teen added.

"Like the contaminated currents of the well?" Susan questioned.

"It is multi-dimensional sorcery," he said.

"I see why those inhabiting the MidEarth have become so poisoned." With a sigh Susan stared into the distance.

"Thank you very much," Eva said as she grabbed the documents from the young man. "See you in a month. Time to get back to Lexington, Susan. We have work to do."

"My name is Yates," he announced. Appearing satisfied that he had been heard, he nodded his head at Susan. "I'll meet you at your shop."

Susan wrinkled her brow. Slightly flustered, she ignored Eva and grabbed her canteen to refill it for the journey. The young man followed her to the well. "I can do that for you. There's a trick to using this well."

Standing close to Susan, he tugged momentarily on the rope above them. There were two ropes hanging over the well. The motion of the top rope brought the second rope within his reach. Using the second rope, he lowered the bucket into the well and drew water. When the bucket filled, he brought it to the top of the well and filled Susan's canteen.

In the dim light of a single lamp, Susan examined the young man's countenance. Accepting the canteen from him she told him, "You seem to know what you are doing. Where do you spend your time when you are not hanging out in the shadows of Boston Commons?"

"I'm a court reporter," he said.

"My second eldest brother worked as a lawyer for the commerce on the Spice Route," Susan mentioned. "He refused to wear a wig because it isolated him from the locals. It also distinguishes him from a British parliamentary group, who named themselves after a fashion statement —- the Whigs."

"I understand," he said. "You'd never know I worked in the courthouse."

"You seem more like a farmer," Susan observed.

"You seem more like a pirate, excuse me, a privateer," he retorted.

Susan's shoulders relaxed as she tied the canteen to her horse. For a moment she turned away and focused on her knot. Casting a sideways glance at Yates, she told him, "That's because I am more of a pirate, at least for the time being. Visit me at the shop in a month, and I'll try to be a shopkeeper." Mounting her horse she said, "Maybe I'll serve you, maybe I won't. Bring more documentation. We'll see."

Then she followed Eva down the trail. Returning to the farm cooperative without incidence, Eva went to the cabin to relieve those caring for Bernie and the captain. Susan hurried to the store where she knew Freddy would be staying. A small back room had been converted into a bedroom. A middle-aged couple with grown children had overseen the shop in her absence and watched Freddy.

While Freddy slept in the back, Susan conversed with the man and woman underneath candlelight.

"The headmaster is very distraught over the deaths of the children," the woman told Susan. "Though he is a Tory, he probably didn't kill his own students."

"None of the children at Freddy's school are ill," the man interjected. "Townsfolk say that he suspects that the British soldiers poisoned the well. Nobody knows for sure."

"People at the Eagles' meeting figured that the school well was contaminated," Susan said. "They said that things like this had happened during the French and Indian War."

"Yes, they did," the woman responded with a firm nod.

"Come in tomorrow," Susan pled. "I want to retrieve the rest of my things from the schoolhouse."

The next day Susan journeyed to the school in Lexington after walking with Freddy to his school. There were no children attending class that day. She entered an empty classroom and found the desk where she kept her texts and writing utensils. As she gathered her things from a desk, the head instructor appeared in the doorway. Startled by his abrupt manner, Susan looked up from her task. He held a clear flask of reddish liquid in his hand.

"Hand over the sunstone necklace or else drink the water from the school well," he said. Then he placed the flask on a shelf. Grabbing his musket from the nearby wall, he raised it to his shoulder and pointed it at her. Aiming to kill, he mentioned, "It has magical powers. I saw its potential for healing when you came for Bernie."

"What's it to you?" Susan questioned. Her back stiffened as she slowly backed away. "It's not magic. It's a symbol of love and devotion. You can't have it."

"Give it to me or else I will contaminate the well at the cooperative," he said. Then he called to the assistant teacher standing outside. "Mr. Larsen, come cut the necklace from Susan's neck."

Brandishing a large knife, Mr. Larsen grabbed Susan from behind, and ripped the necklace from her. Susan gasped, almost choking from the tension in the leather cord. Quickly she regained her breath before they left the room.

She told them as she shook her head, "It won't work for you. You are not an Eagle. You don't have my brothers' blessing."

"What blessing? It will be my cover," the man with the musket said. "I can use it to declare our freedom when war is declared."

Chapter Thirteen

The winter of our lives

Lends itself to greater self-awareness

Reference Tune: *With You I'm Born Again*

----Billy Preston and Syreeta

THE INSTRUCTOR AND his assistant fled with the sunstone necklace. Susan watched them run to their horses and quickly mount them. Then they left for the main road out of town. Several yellow and orange leaves swirled into the air from the horse's hooves. They lingered in the gray, misty autumn air and fell gently behind the desperate men. Susan studied the contrast in motion, and her body lost its tension. Her eyes filled with tears with the release. Throwing her pack over one shoulder, she raced for her favorite tree on the way back to the cooperative. Sitting down on a stout root that had surfaced, she sobbed. Then she went to check on her son at the cooperative.

"Mama," he called when she came. Holding him in her arms, she related the story about the contaminated water supply to the woman who was watching the children. Susan told her about the attack at the schoolhouse. Looking down at her baby's peaceful face, she promised, "I will teach you how to read and write here. You will be safe learning at home."

When she had regained her composure, Susan rose and walked briskly toward the cabin where Eva was caring for the captain. She found the captain walking around the cabin with the aid of a cane. Bernie remained in a semiconscious delirium on his bed nearby. Susan told them what had happened at the schoolhouse. A few tears streaked down the captain's face as Susan confirmed that the drinking water had been contaminated. Eva maintained a poker face under the circumstances. Leaving the couple alone, Susan left to tell the woman watching the shop.

A guard was posted at the well at the cooperative that evening. Freddy remained at the preparatory school for the remainder of the year. Meanwhile, the captain regained his strength and began making plans for the start of the American navy. He went to Boston to meet Marcus and the other half of the crew. Together they plotted their course for the eventual war and the construction of at least ten sloops-of-war. One of the sloops, the Camden, would serve as the captain's vessel, while Marcus retained use of the frigate. Though the meeting only lasted a few days, the sailors accomplished much through their network. Then he returned to the cooperative to care for his dying son.

A few weeks before Thanksgiving, proclaimed by the chamber council in Boston as a public holiday, Yates entered the store with more papers. He politely removed his hat as he stood at the entrance. Catching Susan's eye, he bowed slightly before approaching her.

"I'm sorry about the captain's son," he began. "How far did you get with the reading?" he asked Susan, who was busily wiping the counter.

"I've read the treaties," she answered. "Your story about the water contamination seems to match what we've been seeing here at the farm co-op." Then she said, "Have a seat while I go find Eva. She could use a break and I know that she'd like to see you again."

Moments later, Eva joined Yates at one of the tables. He handed her some documents for her to peruse. Eva briefly studied the papers before her, then stopped and smiled at Yates. Susan remained standing at the counter and brewed some tea for them. Eva didn't say a word. Susan began the discussion while she worked, "We want to know how this War of Regulators fits with the French and Indian War. Eva and I were not impressed by the hospitality of North Carolina."

"The area has become quite hostile," Yates observed. "It is an internal affair. Nobody in New England takes them seriously."

"The land owners, Native Americans, and administrators claim the others are corrupt," Susan said. "We don't think that it is a situation that can be ignored."

"The North Carolina court will decide in the end," Yates contended. "The judge will run off with all the land. My bet is on that horse."

"If that happens, New England will be affected. The judge in North Carolina could war against us." She paused for a moment and gazed at the grains of wood on the bar. Then she asked, "Why do the Native Americans sell out?" Susan asked, leaving the counter to pour tea into their cups.

"Many have died due to bioterrorist techniques perfected in Europe," Yates claimed. "It is as old as the epidemics of ancient Greece. In addition, the Native Americans played both sides of the Seven Years War. Members of the same tribe fought for both England and France. When England won, half of the Native Americans had to surrender. If they had united and fought against both England and France, it might have been a different outcome."

"Were they greedy?" Susan questioned. She sat down in a chair, and looked directly at Yates.

"Sometimes," he responded. "Other times, trading with the enemy comes with huge risks. I don't think the natives understood what hit them."

Then he paused briefly and changed the subject. "Come back to Boston in the spring."

"Why?" she asked.

"Meet some of the sons and daughters of the patriots and Sons of Liberty," he told her. "It is important to know where everyone stands. Positions don't always follow bloodlines."

Rising from his chair, he winked at Susan and exited before she could refuse him. Eva laughed when she saw the wide grin on his face. Susan stood when he ceremoniously walked out the door. Evading Eva's stare, Susan returned to her chair and focused on the aroma rising from her raised tea cup. After one sip, she put the cup down on the table, and rubbed her head. Then she collected the papers on the table.

"We have until spring to get through this reading material," Susan told Eva. "Right now we must take care of our health while caring for loved ones."

Eva, Susan, and the captain continued to rotate shifts for community hospice. In early December, a visitor came to the store while Eva and Susan were working. The tall man leaned over the counter and asked for Eva.

"Who may I say is calling?" Susan asked.

"Daniel Boone," he told her.

Susan shot a glance at Eva, who was hiding behind a curtain. Using makeshift sign language, she waved her hands at Susan to indicate that she wanted more information about the caller. The young man looked in the direction of Susan's gaze, but gave no indication that he knew of Eva's whereabouts.

"What's the nature of your visit with Eva?" Susan questioned.

"I was told that she attended the Eagles's meeting in Boston two months ago. I have additional information for her," he mentioned.

Hearing his words, Eva appeared at the counter and offered the gentleman a seat at a nearby table.

"It's about the war between regulators and the inhabitants in North Carolina," he began as he sat down. "I come from a family of religious dissenters in Pennsylvania. Penn settled them in a colony along with the Quakers. My father was set up as a target there and I am on the run. We are seeing the same scene occur in North Carolina, where political refugees are annihilated to make room for the next parliamentary empire."

"What are you going to do?" Eva asked him. Moved by his story, she lightly touched his hand.

He firmly grasped her fingers in his extended palm and clasped her hand. "Indians in the land ceded by the Stanwix Treaty are being set up for war with the colonies. When England provokes the colonists into a freedom war, the Native Americans will attack from the west. They are under allegiance to the British. The results devastate the Eagles's plans for self-determination."

A tear escaped Eva's eye as she stared beyond the man. It was as if she looked into an abyss, which greedily swallowed lives in its chaotic dynamics. Her reaction brought Susan to the couple.

She interrupted the conversation. Appearing at the table with a pot of tea and several cups, Susan said, "So you are playing Colonel Henderson."

"Correct," Daniel responded, relaxing back in his chair for a better look at Susan. He had joined Eva's stare for a moment and Susan's words jarred his fixed position. A light grin flickered across his countenance.

Filling the cups with a brew, Susan interjected, "When a militia man owns the deed for the land, there will be no peace from the courts. How about using your grass root connections with the Native Americans to fully promote the Quaker notion of goodwill and peace for all?"

Daniel stretched his long legs under the table. He chuckled softly. "What the British soldiers don't know won't hurt us."

"Yes," Susan said. She walked back to the counter, which seemed to nourish her broader perspective on the discussions that took place in the shop. "Make friends with the Native Americans and steer them into neutral territory."

"I had the same idea," he said. "I expect an offer from Henderson for further exploration of the Kentucky region." Then he added, straightening in his chair. "After a brief trip, I shall be able to operate from my place in Concord."

"What brings you here now?" Eva asked.

"My wife recently died from a pox outbreak in Pennsylvania," he said before he released his grip on Eva. "I am here to gather information."

Eva nodded. She related the stories about the epidemic and contaminated wells in the area, also mentioning the skirmish at Green Dragon tavern. Susan listened as she cleaned the area around the counter and straightened shelves. Daniel Boone left shortly after Eva finished. Tipping his hat at both women, he smiled and went outside in the cold.

Bernie died the next week. Heartbroken, the captain departed for New York the day after Christmas. They sold the cabin, and Eva moved in with Freddy and Susan. Several snow storms pounded the cooperative grounds during the first month of the year. The season progressed with continual harsh weather. During the darkest moment, a familiar figure arrived with the bitter wind and opened the door to the store. He removed his hat and elegant scarf by the hearth at the far end of the room. Then he waved a book of poems at Susan.

Remaining motionless behind the counter, she greeted the man loudly so that everyone could hear. "Hello, John Andre! This is a pleasant surprise. Eva, you have an admirer."

Eva dried her hands in the small kitchen and ran to him. Freddy popped out from an empty cupboard where he had been playing. Without any formalities, Eva hugged him and kissed his cheek. Freddy bounced on his feet and leaped in front of him. John Andre caught him in midair, lifting him to his shoulders.

"If I had known what kind of reception waited me, I would have come sooner," he said with a smile. "I have come to help the Eagles." Waving at Susan, who poured him a mug of tea from behind the counter, he said, "Marcus sends his regards."

"How is he?" she asked bringing the warm brew over to him.

"He told me everything," John Andre said wrapping his arm around Eva. "The captain is not in the best of spirits these days."

Chapter Fourteen

Don't give up on a dream

Too soon

Reference Tune: *Don't Dream It's Over*

----Crowded House

FOR A MOMENT John Andre gazed into Eva's brown eyes. Then he surveyed the store as he placed Freddy on the floor. The young boy playfully tugged at John Andre's pockets before draping his arms around the man's torso. Extending a free arm, he invited Susan to share their embrace. Susan obliged him and joined the huddle. After releasing the three people around him, he sat down at a table by the hearth. Slouching in his chair, he said, "It is a bitter January. I learned many things while in the service conducting war in Germany. My education in the British armed forces taught me that the action is here."

Freddy fetched a bowl of curry from the kitchen. Placing it before John Andre, he asked, "What brings you here now?"

"Why, you do," John Andre replied, lifting Freddy on his lap. "I met the captain enlisting men for this continent's navy. He requested that I escort you to New York so that you could begin the new school year."

He paused to sip his tea and collect his breath. Everyone gathered around him remained wordless, cultivating an awkward silence that compelled Andre to continue his story. He obliged their awed state. "I told the captain that I could do better than that. I said that I was going to take Freddy in." Then he started eating his meal and spoke between bites as if no one else heard him. "Under orders of the captain, I am escorting Freddy to his new home in New York. He will stay with me, Major John Andre, while he is on leave from the British forces in Canada. Before the revolution is declared, I will escort Freddy, the Prince, to Nova Scotia under the protection of the American navy. From Canada, we will catch a frigate back to England where he will rejoin his younger brother. In this manner, the prince will be hidden from the designs of the British parliament on the royal family."

Nobody interrupted the major. Freddy hopped off John Andre's lap and faced him directly. John Andre stopped eating and turned around. Looking Freddy in the eye, he continued as he placed a hand on his soldier. "Freddy, it is important that our royals become as free as the American colonies. Your father's enemies have already taken your older brother as their protégé. Perhaps they have something to do with king's present derangement. Like the rest of us in this room, Freddy, you have a chance for freedom too. You can escape the crazed powers of the Roman Empire that are seizing the monarchies."

"Tell us more," Eva pled.

"There are two types of colonists. There are those who need a monarchy for the sake of order, and those who sympathize with the royals because they already have a sense of order."

"Apparently, the hysteria is past the point of no return," Susan observed.

"Apparently," John Andre repeated. "I learned this in Germany. We first saw the symptom in India, when brother was incited against brother. It is not an easy job rescuing a prince from relations that intend to kill him."

"I appreciate your help," Freddy said. "We will be friends forever."

"In the meanwhile," John Andre added. "Keep me away from the British soldiers. They think that I work for them. For all they know, I am visiting government administrators in New York." Patting Freddy assuredly on the shoulder before returning to his dinner, he contended, "I am a Loyalist, but not by the definition of the British forces intending to sabotage Freddy."

"When do you leave?" Eva questioned.

"Early tomorrow morning," John Andre replied. "Both Freddy and I must escape detection. Everyone except the American navy believes that Freddy lives in some boring castle in England."

The next morning, Freddy said good-bye to Eva and Susan. Taking John Andre's hand, he exited through the front door into the snowy dawn. John Andre tipped his hat to the young women.

"I will be back," he told them. "We are just beginning."

No one shed a tear as the group split up into two. Susan shook her head and added, "Thanks for bringing us hope in the midst of such loss." Then she glanced at a pendulum clock hanging on the wall. She commented, "It will be time for business in a few hours. Best of luck to you and your travels."

Two months later, the Sons of Liberty provoked a British attack on civilians. Although the incident did not result in a declaration of war, the colonists called it a massacre. The British soldiers were tried in a courthouse near the homestead of the first recognized American refugees.

"The father of one of the Eagles is representing the British soldiers," Yates told them during his next visit. "The colonists are getting emotional about the event. Crowds are congregating around the trial at Plymouth Rock."

"Was she at the meeting last October?" Eva questioned.

"No, she keeps a low profile around the Commons," Yates answered. "She is known by her mother's nickname. The Eagles call her Nabby." Eyeing Susan, he said, "Come to Boston, and I'll introduce you to the others. Spring is here."

Rising from his chair, he slightly bowed before Susan. With a nod in Eva's direction, he walked out of the store.

The next month, Eva came down with the fever. Susan cared for her along with the other three, while she hired two people to run the shop. Their group earned enough profit to leave the operation of the place in the hands of others in the cooperative and hire those who needed the additional income.

"It must be the absence of the sunstone necklace that contributed to your vulnerability," Susan commented as she bathed Eva's forehead with wet compresses. "People suspect that the former schoolmaster contaminated the well. He carried out his threat despite the theft."

Eva looked at Susan with dark brown eyes and shuddered. With trembling hands, she untied her necklace and handed it to Susan. Nobody spoke. Susan studied the object in her hands for a moment. Glancing at the reflections in Eva's irises, she retied the crystal to her own neck. She told Eva, "We'll see what good this thing does now. The townspeople determined that the head teacher was a sorcerer for the Roman Empire, whereas his assistant associated with a group of occultists from the underground of Solomon's Temple. Apparently the guilds have joined forces with the British soldiers."

Eva recovered two weeks later. She helped Susan care for the others, who had become ill. The next month British soldiers arrived in town. They searched the homes and farms for weapons and militia, entering the hospice area while several soldiers began inspecting the beds.

"Who is this?" one red coat questioned. He pried the mattress with his bayonet, barely missing the bedridden young man. "Why aren't you drilling like the rest?"

Then the soldier put his bayonet aside and choked the man to death. Susan stepped outside to retrieve her musket. Firing a few shots in the air, she succeeded in scaring away the soldiers, who could not see who had fired the gun. They scurried out of the buildings and mounted their horses.

Hiding behind a cabin as they turned their horse around, Susan overheard their conversation. The soldiers panicked, and their horses became confused. The stallions refused to obey the orders.

"Who fired?" one red coat gasped.

"I don't know," answered another.

Hearing their words, Susan fired another round in the air and bounced some of the bullets off a metal tub. The sound made the location of the shooter indistinct. The riders regained control of their steeds.

"Let's get out of here. We are under orders not to shoot," the soldier who had murdered her patient remarked. "We don't want to lead Britain into an undeclared war. Not yet."

The red coats galloped away. Susan returned to the hospice to care for the traumatized patients and bury the dead man. Some other members of the farming cooperative came to help. Eva began moving the hospice into a more secure location. Someone had offered a room near their cellar to hide the recovering people.

Yates appeared at the store the next morning. This time he had a minuteman with him. The man was almost ten years older than Yates, and he had been selected by the townsfolk of Concord to protect them. "Hi, my name is Isaac Davis."

Yates grinned wryly at Susan. "The British soldiers are getting antsy. The latest letter of Junius rattled them. The English courts are allowing the papers to denigrate the Crown. The town of Lexington has drafted you as a minutewoman."

Chapter Fifteen

It's fourth down in a game of football
And you are ninety-five yards from your goal
Time to punt
Get the ball away from your opponent's goal
And send out an S.O.S

Reference Tune: *Message In A Bottle*
----The Police

SUSAN PLACED HER hands on her hips. "Is this what you do between visits? Drill with the renegade armed forces?"

"They killed our best sergeant," the minuteman quipped. "His death was avenged. The fleeing horses reared on the British soldiers, killing three of the officers. I don't think the red coats will continue to murder the sick in their homes anymore. They are sending fresh, inexperienced soldiers to the continent."

Yates added, "The British soldiers are getting rattled by the latest letter of Junius. The English courts are allowing newspapers to print the letters. They support the hellfire king of libel, John Wilkes."

"The problem is that the radical is a hypocrite," the minuteman added. "Wilkes really wants the keys to the Bank of England."

Susan sat down on a nearby chair and scratched her head. Then she rose to find Eva. Finding her stirring several pots in the kitchen, Susan asked,

"Eva, can you and the hired help cover for me while I go to Boston tomorrow? Give me about two months to catch up on looming legalities, and work on a greater business network for the store. We need to preserve our commercial interests as well."

Susan sensed that she had overheard the conversation in the store. Eva never looked up from the cook top. "Leave it me. Don't forget to bring the pink dress."

The following evening, Yates and the minuteman met Susan at the back of the store. They rode under the cover of darkness to avoid arousing the suspicion of roving British soldiers. A family from Lexington with relations in Boston rode ahead with Greg. He stayed in the city, while Susan made other arrangements. When they reached Boston, Susan obtained room and board at an inn near Faneuil Hall.

"Come join us for dinner in the smaller room near the dining hall. I want to introduce you to Sam Adams before we make the social rounds. He is the only politician we trust in Massachusetts," Yates told her, while placing several of her bags in the room. "I will be down the hall if you need me. See you at seven tonight."

Removing his hat, he watched Susan's expression as he closed the door between them. Her eyes were wide with the evolving changes in scenery around her. She stood in the doorway like a refined porcelain doll spinning around to the music from a jewelry box. Locking the door behind him, she immediately unpacked her pink dress and hung it. For a moment, she smoothed out the wrinkles while gazing into the lacy patterns defining the garment.

In the evening, she put on a fresh skirt and blouse before descending the stairs to the dining room. The men in the room rose when she entered.

Behind the youthful looking Yates and seasoned gentlemen, stood the vibrant Mr. Adams. He rushed over to shake her hand as Yates made introductions.

"Please, come meet my relation, Nabby Adams," Sam told her. He pushed a young woman in front of Susan. Composing herself before acknowledging anyone in the room, she exclaimed to Susan, "Nice to meet you! We have lots to talk about."

Susan grinned at their exuberance. Surveying the present occupants in the room before sitting down at the table, she whispered to Yates, "There aren't many women present. Are there any more coming?"

"Nabby is the great connector, and unlike Sam, the most reliable in these parts," Yates said. "Let her link you to the others. You'll need an ally."

After a few introductory comments, the conversation focused on Lexington's runaway school instructor and his assistant.

What was the significance of the sunstone necklace?" Sam asked.

Susan pulled the leather strings of the necklace from underneath her blouse. Exposing the pendant to those in the room, she turned the crystal in her palm until she obtained the desired reflection. Isaac and Yates listened intently, while Susan explained how Da Vinci and the others had created a special knighthood to protect world commerce. "They were called the Eagles. The stolen pendant looked like this one in my hands. The two fitted together to make a single ornament."

"Yes, we are being closely watched by the eye-in-the-sky," Sam commented as he glanced at the necklace.

"Who?" Nabby questioned. "The aliens?

"Evidently," Sam replied. "The eye-in-the-sky gang is just one of the four races of aliens. They pertain to the Black Dog occult group from ancient

Egypt. The large pyramid keeps an eye on them. They were from Sirius, the dog star."

"Who are the others?" Nabby asked.

"The Gauds and their M33 intermediaries comprise one group. The M33 group pertains to a particular galaxy of large arachnids that spin webs of religious fervor. The Grays count as a separate race now. The Serpentines constitute the fourth race. The alien races work together as a large family, though they sometimes have disagreements."

"Our latest concerns are the Boston riots and massacre," Isaac interjected. "None of these incidents were condoned by the state militia or minutemen."

"Now that we have minutewomen, we have minute forces," Yates interrupted.

"Yes, we are adding a magical element to the armies protecting the continent," Isaac rejoined. "We intend to treat our alliances with France and the Eagles with respect."

"Well said," Sam remarked. "I'll have my cousin John work with the French while we keep the Eagles here. In fact, we should all become Eagles and counter the present occultism in world commerce."

The minuteman continued, "At the Governor's party tomorrow night, we request that you press for removal of British occupation."

"I agree," Sam told them. "I'll add that to my list of repeals."

"There's a bigger picture," Yates said. "The privateers tell me that Britain is releasing fifty-thousand convicts. They are in the boats heading for our shores as we speak. Don't mention this to the governors. We don't need another excuse for the British to stay in our homes."

"We'll have to come up with something else," Isaac said. "No more crying to our British parents. We want an independent nation. They mustn't throw the baby out with the bath water."

"This brings us back to the Eagles," Sam said, looking Susan directly in the eye. "We don't want to be fed to the alien masters like our European parents."

"Yes, we saw that happen in India," Susan said. "What do you have in mind?"

"Come to the governor's party and help me plead my case," Sam answered. "I trust that you brought formal attire."

"Yes, my friend made sure that I came prepared for anything," Susan rejoined.

The dinner ended shortly thereafter. People left separately for their rooms to minimize suspicion.

"No crowds here for British soldiers to fear," Susan said as Yates escorted her back to her room.

"No," he said, anxiously turning his head from side to side. The hall remained vacant behind them. No footsteps could be heard from the stairwells at both ends of the hall. "I'll pick you up at four in the afternoon for the occasion. How about having brunch with Nabby and myself as we go over documents? It would be a great way to brief before being entertained by the governor and his company. Meet us at the diner in Faneuil Hall. Then we'll go to my office."

At brunch the next morning, Susan repeated a phrase uttered by Isaac. "There's a bigger picture," she began as she sat down across from Nabby and Yates. Several of Yates's aides were also in the diner, which seemed conspicuously empty for a bustling trade center.

"We had the place reserved for administrative business," Yates explained when he noticed the perplexed expression on Susan's face. We won't be long. We can finish in my office."

"As I said, there's a bigger picture," she echoed, seeming satisfied with the reason for the relatively calm environment. She leaned toward Nabby and Yates as if taking them in her confidence. "Have you thought about how the country started with being a haven for religious and political refugees, and the next move is to fill it with thieves and murderers?"

"Hmm," Yates said, cocking his head from side to side. He smiled at Susan in reply.

"You have a point," Nabby responded in a hushed voice.

Susan continued, "So what would be the next step for the irresponsible European parents?"

Yates grinned and scratched his head.

"That's a good one," Nabby commented, leaning closer to Susan like she was in a huddle. "What do you think?"

"We are being bullied for exploitation," she said. "Regardless of who controls Parliament or the monarchy or the planet, we are in trouble. There is nothing left for us, except freedom and strength."

Yates firmly thumped his fist on the table. Nabby eagerly nodded, warming herself by rubbing her arms and hands. She glanced around the room to study the reaction of those who had been listening. People blinked and smiled.

"We are going to have to break Sam in gently," Yates concluded. "He still thinks that we should stick with George III."

"Not after I witnessed the barbarism in India with the assassination of extended royal family," Susan said.

"You're right," Nabby said with a final decisive nod before looking at Yates. "So what are we going to do?"

"Work with Sam. He'll steer Hancock and some of the other politicians," Yates concluded. "Meanwhile, we must gather our notes and present our case with subtlety. Like the minutemen or minute forces, a little bit goes a long way. Sometimes all it takes is one deadly shot."

"Are you referring to the Hancock living in Lexington?" Susan questioned.

"Yes, Hancock is the wealthy merchant who owned the Liberty. British soldiers asserted their command of his commerce. However, he sidestepped Sam's call for a boycott of British goods. Sam learned how to herd politicians like cattle. There's more safety in numbers."

They finished their meal and then adjourned to Yates's office for further studies. Afterwards, the group dispersed to prepare for the governor's occasion. Yates escorted Susan to the mansion, and gracefully deposited her by Sam's side.

"What is your business?" an astute wigged man asked her."

"Commerce," Susan replied. "I run a shop between Lexington and Concord. We sell various spiced goods and sundries obtained from the traders in Boston Harbor." Then she stared at the governor and his staff, "Surely the British troops would have greater effect on the West coast where illicit religious orders are baptizing the natives against us as part of their mission."

The governor bowed slightly at Susan when he heard her remark.

Sam added, "Where there are Spanish, there is gold."

Turning to Susan, the governor mentioned, "Go talk with some of the dealers here. The British appreciate their commercial interests in America. Here, let my associate show you around."

Susan accompanied the governor's man around the party and cultivated many potential customers. At some point during the gathering, someone directed them to a man standing in a corner with another group. "That's John Hancock. He lives near you. You should both meet."

"Oh, are you at that little farm near the North Bridge?" Hancock questioned with a slight sneer.

Susan backed away. "Yes, we are expanding. Come in sometime and add a little spice to your life."

Hancock laughed as she politely left to find Yates. Spotting him at the opposite end of the hall, she whispered in his ear, "Let's go before I wear out my welcome."

He chuckled and feigned good humor. Leaning back and standing upright, he said loudly. "Yes, my sentiments exactly. Fellows, I have court duty early tomorrow morning. If you please excuse us, I must prepare for the legal proceedings."

Two months later, Yates and Isaac went with Susan back to the cooperative. Greg and his caretakers planned to return to Lexington a few days after they left. Without checking on her places elsewhere, Susan entered the store and found Eva working the kitchen. Eva dried her hands and hugged Susan in greeting. Yates and Isaac tipped their hat in greeting, quickly departing for business in Concord as the women conversed in private.

"You've been busy," Susan commented as she held Eva's hand to acknowledge the ring around her finger.

Before Susan could say another word, Eva explained, "Mr. Daniel Boone confronted me on my relationship with the captain. I told him that the captain is still heartbroken over the loss of his son and wife. Death drove us apart. It proved just a short-lived fling. Then Daniel proposed last week. He is over his loss, and so am I."

Susan sat down on a nearby chair and relaxed for the first time since spring.

Chapter Sixteen

Teleportation

And the sinking of the Edmund Fitzgerald

Reference Tune: *Wreck Of The Edmund Fitzgerald*

----Gordon Lightfoot

AS A RESULT of Susan's networking and Eva's connections with the scouting community, the cooperative shop prospered. Daniel Boone frequented the store, and made plans with Eva concerning their wedding in the year 1773. Susan continued working with Yates and the others. Often they could be seen on long walks around the fields discussing the latest political designs. Other times, the community of minute forces could be seen drilling around the grounds.

One cold, rainy late afternoon in November of 1771, Freddy burst into the shop and ran to the counter. He announced, "We're back!"

Eva appeared from the adjacent kitchen and drew back the curtain partition. Daniel Boone emerged from behind her and studied the exuberant youth. Susan entered the shop through the front door with a load of supplies in her arms.

"There you are!" she yelled to Freddy. "I found John Andre tying up the horses in the barn. He's on his way."

Freddy ran over to help Susan. Relieving her of some objects, he announced, "Aliens attacked Staten Island, so we decided to leave New York and go to England later."

John Andre appeared in the room. He took off his hat and began unbuttoning his jacket by the hearth. "The group that has been watching us from Sirius destroyed several homes in the area. This time we managed to hit one of their flying ships. A man by the name of Ellis downed the spaceship and had it moved to Oyster Island. Marcus O'Connor, your former captain on the frigate, summoned benevolent extraterrestrials for help. We didn't want a repeat of what we endured in India."

"Where's Captain Drake?" Eva questioned.

John Andre sighed and plopped down in a chair. He raised one eyebrow as Daniel Boone joined him by the hearth. Then he looked at Susan, who only offered him a noncommittal shrug. Both Daniel and Eva made themselves comfortable around Andre while Susan brought over a tray of refreshments before grabbing a seat. Freddy opted to sit as close as possible to Susan without being in her lap. Everyone waited for Andre to answer.

"He's coming," John Andre said. "He's been sailing with Marcus, and establishing connections with Ison."

"Ison is the name of the extraterrestrial ship," Freddy interjected, bouncing in his chair. "Some people think it is a comet."

"Captain Drake convinced Ellis to purchase the island and use the alien ship as a tavern trophy," John Andre explained. "He wants to move the headquarters for the Green Dragon underground here. He plans to convert the shop into a tavern."

Before Susan had a chance to respond, Eva confronted her, "There's something you should know. You've been in the dark about what has been happening around you. Robert has protected you from what has been happening in the Continental Navy."

"Let me guess," Susan countered. "It has something to do with John Paul Jones and the Lycee Republican or College of Apollo."

Eva sat back in her chair and took Daniel's hand. "That's another alien group associated with the M33 occultists and Gauds."

Without a word, Susan looked up from her task and glanced at the ceiling, searching for a sense of reassurance. "I don't understand how I fit into the captain's scheme."

"Which brings us to the importation of a third alien group," John Andre interrupted. "Both royal houses of Stuart and Hanover have the same underground, which is being feathered into the major cities with the Hessians and convicts. They have Sicilian connections as far back as Da Vinci's time. There is a reason one monarch was called Bloody Mary, and her surviving network is arriving in the harbors for business. These networks have been heavily influenced by their Salic relations, who abide by laws that don't make any sense anymore." Moving closer to the couple, John Andre leaned forward in his chair. He added, "One of the laws specifies that the heirs must be male. Henry the VIII gave us two female contenders for the thrones of Europe."

A shudder ran through Daniel Boone's spine and he squirmed in his seat. He told Eva, "Like some of our effected Native Americans, these alien groups distinguish themselves through ritual murder. The purpose is spiritual annihilation through barbaric torture," Daniel added, uncomfortably shuffling his legs while remaining seated in his chair.

"Well, so much for commerce," Susan stated, ducking underneath the counter again to rearrange stacks of dishes and cups. "Next thing, rowdies will be dumping tea in Boston Harbor."

"Don't give them any more ideas," Freddy told Susan.

"I won't," Susan retorted as she rose to refill her cup. "The old head instructor will probably put the Sons of Liberty up to it. I think he mentioned it in a lesson, as he thought out-loud."

"No wonder the British soldiers pushed on him," Freddy commented.

"I'm going to check with Yates," Susan said. After putting on her boots and coat, she kissed John Andre affectionately on the cheek. She asked him, "Please join us for musket drills tomorrow. We could use your expertise."

John Andre smiled at her. "Yes, we will be joined by young Mr. Nathan Hale. I have been working with him. His friend, Daniel Smith, will be with him. Smith and the captain are attempting to establish another tavern in Philadelphia."

"Yes, more are coming," Daniel Boone continued. "I expect Mr. John Gibson, an agent with Native American affairs to join us next week."

"Robert is using his Green Dragon network to protect you, Susan," Eva told her.

"Sam Adams intends to turn America into a country of Eagles," Susan responded. "I'm not so sure about those Sons of Liberty." Wrapping a scarf around her neck before opening the door, she continued, "And I am not sure why the Sicilian ruffians are targeting me."

"Let's hope Sam Adams succeeds before Ben Franklin and John Paul Jones make us turkeys," John Andre commented. He stood and gently stopped Susan before she opened the door. Straightening the scarf covering the necklace, he explained, "The Davenports of New Rochelle in New York want control of the time wrinkle. Their family crest has a man with a rope around his neck. For centuries, they have wanted to decide who lives and who dies. The powers of this necklace save you. You are the Eagle that got away. You helped us all escape the time wrinkle in India."

Susan looked at him directly in the eye. Calmly, she told him, "I see. It's about free choice and free will." With a light wave of her hand, she left the group to consult Yates.

Instead of meeting Yates, who had left for business in a nearby town, Susan went to the home that she shared with Nathan. Daniel Smith, a representative from Annapolis, and Nathan were already there. Daniel Smith handed her Greg, whom he had been entertaining in her absence. Using his culinary skills as a cover, Daniel Smith worked with the collection of artisans from the Andromeda galaxy, who presently resided at Althorp with the Spencers in England.

Susan told them the latest news from the cooperative store. "I suspect that Yates will ask me to accompany him to Philadelphia. There's more work to do on the documents and he has access to Benjamin Franklin's library." Playfully shaking her head at Greg, she remarked, "There's an ideological muscle behind Yates. Someone else is doing the legal work; Yates is covering for another person."

"My cook's family can help watch Greg while you are in town," Daniel Smith replied. "I am establishing a base of operations for the Freedom Trail there. We can easily care for one more baby there."

Two weeks later, the captain arrived and immediately began construction of the tavern, which they named after the leading family in the cooperative. Daniel Boone left for a scouting mission in the nearby woods, while John Gibson arrived and conversed with Susan over Native American affairs. They formulated an agenda similar to Daniel Boone's, which amounted to forming allies with Native Americans. Susan used Gibson's connections in the northern part of the country to enlist the aid of the Iroquois Confederacy, which already had a system of government established amongst five tribes. She and Yates fed Sam Adams ideas on the creation of a strong and free nation.

During the spring of 1772, the underground from an Italian ghetto in Boston approached the barn where Susan milked Matilda. Matilda alerted Susan to the attackers by a series of uncharacteristic low moans. As she stood to retrieve a sword hanging from the adjacent wall, two men blindfolded her from behind. Without a moment's hesitation, Susan reached for the sword with one hand while grabbing the hilt of the sword from one attacker. Releasing the second sword from its sheath, she kicked one man in the groin and elbowed the other in the ribs. Then she swirled both swords around her like two rapidly moving batons leading a parade. The seven men moved away to avoid being sliced by the deadly circles she wove around herself. Matilda kicked one man in the shin and he cried loudly in unexpected pain. The noise drew the attention of the men working on the tavern.

Chapter Seventeen

No harm in dancing

Even if it is just for a moment

Reference Tune: *Dance With Me*

----Orleans

THE CAPTAIN HEARD the distress calls of the milk cow followed by a masculine yelp. He dropped his tools and hurried to the barn with his sword drawn. Freddy and Nathan ran behind him with their weapons. Entering the barn as a collective unit, they immediately slew the seven men around Susan. Freddy ran his sword through the man rubbing his broken leg. He died instantly. Nathan killed two men and wounded a third. Freddy completed the kill of the wounded man, while the captain slaughtered the remaining three. A hanging rope fell out of the pocket of the last attacker to fall.

Susan stopped the circular motion with the swords when the sound of clashing metal and voices ceased. Untying the blindfold, she witnessed the collapse of the executioner several yards from her feet. Her eyes widened as she gasped at the sight.

"It looks like they knew what they were doing," she said as she stooped over to collect the rope. "We can sell this for profit. Burn the bodies. We don't want anyone digging this up."

Then she unleashed Matilda from her stall and took the cow for a walk. First, she threw the rope on the store porch for resale, then she took off to her favorite grove of trees. Matilda softly mooed beside her. Freddy followed behind her for a few steps and then pulled back. He went inside the tavern in search of Eva.

"Thanks Freddy," she softly said before he left.

"You're bleeding!" the captain yelled at Susan.

Eva appeared in front of her with a rag, while the captain stayed with the others to clean the barn and discretely dispose of the evidence. Susan paused to examine the possible source of blood on her neck. Matilda turned her head and licked Susan on the neck.

"There," Eva said, brushing Matilda's snout aside to dab the cuts. "Two shallow incisions placed equal distance apart on different sides of the neck."

"Looks like a ritual murder; tastes like a ritual murder," Susan responded as she addressed Matilda.

The cow mooed in protest and turned her head in the direction of several plants growing nearby.

"The leather string of the necklace stopped their swords," Eva remarked wiping the blood off the leather. The necklace remained untouched and did not require cleaning.

"Odd," Susan commented. "I thought that it was in my skirt pocket. I had taken it off for a quick swim."

Matilda continued to moan and toss her head in the direction of the plants. Susan looked at the restless cow.

"Look, Eva!" Susan cried. "Some styptics are growing in that patch of red clover. I'll munch on the head of the red flower. Please, put the Robert geranium on the neck."

Eva reached for the plants. "Robert geranium will dry things up."

"It looks like we've hit bottom," Susan commented. "We must be moving out of the crisis that began in India."

Susan released the leash on Matilda, who began feasting on wild edibles. After reconnecting with her feelings while in the grove, Susan returned to the barn. Eva went back to the shop to keep watch. The men had already scavenged and gathered the bodies for a pyre. While they quickly restored order, Susan picked up the attacker's swords left on the ground. She spied an engraving on the hilt that was most polished.

Taking the sword with her to confer with the others, she approached the men piling the bodies. "I recognize the words carved into this sword. It belonged to the family of Comte Caliostro, a descendant of Sauron's wizardry forays in Narni. They work with the Davenports."

"I see the connection to the MidEarth," the captain related. He waved for the others to examine the dead more closely for further clues. "They are Sauron's family of dark knights. It is a world-wide organization."

"Who was Sauron?" Nathan questioned. He stood erect to catch his breath after a final search yielded no further information.

"Who is Sauron?" Freddy rejoined. He patted Nathan's shoulder after a gentle tug. "Sauron is the immortal vampire that haunts the halls of monarchies since the end of King Arthur's reign. He makes people's heads go crazy."

"Our friends in the MidEarth subdued him during the intergalactic wars of ancient Egypt," the captain told Nathan. "Susan serves as our ambassador to the MidEarth, and she travels between here and there through a portal."

"Things have changed," Susan remarked to Nathan. "Besides the spaceship Ison, the MidEarth inhabitants are our allies. Ison will protect the skies while the MidEarth inhabitants assume human form to help establish a free nation on the earth plane."

Nathan listened for a second, then looked down at Freddy. His eyes searched for more information from the prince. Freddy returned Nathan's stare with a slight smile.

"I am an Eagle," he mentioned to Nathan when she was out of earshot." Susan has been teaching me. She told me that she needs all the help she can get. Only two of the little people will remain in the MidEarth to help with the transport of souls into the next life."

"The hauflins?" Nathan questioned. He nodded his head in recognition. "I want to become better acquainted with the Eagles and Susan."

"Yes, the hauflins," Freddy said before he got back to work.

Chapter Eighteen

Don't you just hate it when---?

Reference Tune: *Wildfire*

----Michael Martin Murphey

THREE DAYS LATER, Yates and a friend arrived from Boston. The gentleman resembled Sam Adams in many ways, except he appeared only four years older than Yates and much leaner than Sam. His muscular frame suggested that he spent less time in politics and more time working on a farm.

"Isaac Davis sent a message about the attack. You must come to Philadelphia with me and Joseph," he told Susan. "The change of scenery will do you good. The rest of the gang may come around looking for their members."

Joseph bowed slightly and took Susan's hand. "My half-brother Sam said that you could help us in Pennsylvania."

"I'm meeting all the relations of Sam Adams. He must have a large extended family," Susan remarked.

"Not really," he said. "Sam and I think the same, which separates us from the other Boston Brahmins."

"You must tell me more on the trip," Susan responded. "Being a Brahmin, you must be familiar with my brothers' work."

"Somewhat," Joseph replied. "We heard about the Eagles knighthood from sailor's tales. We are happy that you blew to this continent in time for Sam's Committee of Correspondence."

"That's why we need you in Philadelphia," Yates said. "We are setting up a shadow government in case the British lay siege to Boston."

"Doesn't Boston already have a shadow government?" Susan questioned.

"That's why we must set up another in Philadelphia," Yates quipped. "In case, they come after us."

They arrived in Philadelphia before the summer of 1772. They stayed at a housing complex on Market Street. Down the street, Deborah Reed and her three year old grandson held court in the absence of her common-law husband, Benjamin Franklin. Franklin remained in England, and missed the birth of his grandson, whom Deborah affectionately called Benny. Already well-acquainted with the work of the Eagles, she brought together delegates from a variety of places.

"She is the best teacher around," Joseph commented before they knocked on the door to her home. "The action is in Franklin Court, not at the Pennsylvania State House."

"When Deborah dies, they'll be moving Franklin Court there and calling it Independence Hall," Yates added. "It is all happening under Franklin's nose. He'll have to go with the flow when he returns."

"When is that?" Susan questioned.

"Nobody knows. The legislators keep extending his stay," Yates said as they waited for the door to open.

"Any particular reason?" Susan asked.

"Politics," Joseph said with a wide grin. He shrugged with feigned ignorance.

Benny answered the door. The young toddler curiously examined the youthful group from head to toe.

"It's okay, Benny. Let them in," a woman in her early sixties said bustling behind the toddler.

She stooped over and picked up the small lad in her arms. He smiled at the visitors as she ushered them toward the library-study. When he saw where the group was heading, Benny almost leapt from her. Deborah quickly put his feet on the ground, and the small boy raced to the room ahead of them.

"Smart boy," Joseph commented. "We have plenty of work to do."

Closing the door behind them in the room, Deborah perched down on a large burgundy chair. Benny sat on the floor at her feet and began playing with some lettered wood blocks. The others remained standing as they browsed through the collection of books and documents.

"Pennsylvania enjoyed reading the Eagle's Bill of Rights," Deborah amiably began. "The colonists want more."

"What do you mean 'more'?" Joseph asked, procuring a book from the shelf with her wordless consent.

"We want a constitution for the event," she replied.

Benny looked up from his alphabet blocks and stared at his grandmother. He glanced at Yates, who was studying the legal papers on the nearby desk.

Scarcely looking up, Yates echoed, "What event?"

"The event when we declare ourselves independent," Deborah replied.

Benny returned his attention to his toys as Yates turned over the pages of the documents on the desk. The room quieted except for the sound of shuffling papers from the desk. Joseph began hurriedly thumbing through the book in his hands. Susan stood and watched the scene. Eventually she focused on Deborah's placid expression as Yates answered in the monotone of a legal voice.

"That is more than just a matter of legalization."

"I should be the one to know," Deborah continued.

"Do you think you and Franklin will ever marry?" Joseph asked pointedly.

"Not on my life," she said. "Benny and I are having too much fun here."

Yates looked up from the documents on the desk. He studied Deborah's poker face, while Joseph directed Susan to another book on the shelf. Climbing a small ladder, he grabbed the heavy text from a top shelf and passed it down to her.

"We'll need to hide the documents until the proper moment. Meanwhile, we'll lead the others on a Fox hunt, and establish a provisional government, which must be in place for the shadow governments to come out of hiding. Otherwise, we will lose everything."

"My sentiments, exactly, except there is no sentiment," Deborah responded.

"Exactly!" Joseph exclaimed as he closed a book excitedly.

Deborah silently nodded, but her eyes shone with determination. "Leave the fox hunting to the Philadelphia gentry, like my penniless son-in-law in the local club. Fox hunting in this city is a passionless pit."

Susan drew Joseph aside and asked, "Is the reference double-fold? Captain Drake mentioned that Fox had been appointed on the Admiral's Board, but had quit due to personal legitimacy issues."

"The reference is threefold," Joseph said with a merry air.

Deborah winked at Susan in affirmation.

Yates interjected, "Though Fox is the fervent parliamentary power opposing the monarchy, the speculation is that he intends to promote the colonies with his family's request for earldom."

"They expect the war with the colonies to do the job," Joseph added. "The substitution of one king for another does nothing for America, no matter how patriotic these people appear on the surface."

Yates counted on his fingers as Deborah mimicked his gesture for Benny's further education. "One is fox, the crafty animal hunted for mere sport. Two is Fox, the worthless politician bent on violence for personal gain. Three is the fox club, chock-full of worthless patriots who sway on the edge of a schilling."

Awed by the degree of wit in the room, Susan proposed, "It makes the case for legitimacy of a new government on this continent."

"So the Eagles don't get burnt in a three-way script," Yates said.

Joseph added, "The reference is at least threefold, but the metaphor will serve for the moment."

For the duration of the summer, they worked in Franklin's office and in the local legislative offices. They combed through papers and legal precedences to chart their way. More serious than a high-wire act in a circus, they determined to win with a decisive air and foolproof structure. Only one incident proved a distraction.

"I can't believe those red squirrels got away with running the British ship aground at Gaspee Point, Rhode Island," Yates commented when he brought the news to the library.

"We've gone from foxes to red squirrels," Susan observed.

"We want to stay out of the setup, especially since the matter is being brought to Fox," Joseph mentioned, continuing to thumb through the book in his hands. "Squirrel is an off-hand term for case without any substance. These cases win because they are structural sound, and usually too unusual to refute."

"Sometimes madness wins," Susan commented.

"Sometimes," Joseph said. "Then there are greasers. Greasers slip everything through the system whether they should or not."

By the end of the summer, Susan had picked up enough information to find her way through any legal matter, much less the documentation of a new government.

"It is time to learn from the opposition," Yates told Susan one afternoon. "You and I have been invited to dinner at the City Tavern. The people of Pennsylvania just approved the construction. It is on the site of an older establishment."

"How formal?" Susan asked.

"We will be meeting George Read from the Delaware assembly, William Samuel Johnson, who has just been appointed to the colony's Supreme Court, and Gouverneur Morris, Johnson's political protégé from King's College."

"What about me?" Joseph questioned with a mock rhetorical air.

Slapping Joseph on the shoulders in jest, Yates told him, "You get to remain a virtual unknown as the half-brother of Sam Adams."

"That's what happens when you look like Sam Adams," Joseph joked. "A younger version really scares the legislators."

On the evening of the dinner, Yates and Susan walked over to City Tavern. Although she wore the pink dress, she did not express concern about exposing it to the city grime. The warm, early autumn weather kept the streets clean. Choosing to linger in the fresh air, they decided against taking a carriage.

When they arrived at the tavern, the three legislators greeted them and immediately ushered them to a round table inside.

"This conflict with England has brought us all to the brink of revolution," George Read began.

"How much longer do you think it will take to establish a new government?" Samuel Johnson asked.

Yates sidestepped the question and ordered a cup of tea. Noticing his abrupt departure from the conversation, Susan responded with a question, "What revolution? I thought we already had a new government with all the reforms in England."

George leaned closer to the couple and looked them directly in the eye. "I am talking about the changes in the governance of the British colonies."

"Changes? Has there been any change?" Susan asked.

"Yates, where have you been keeping Susan?" Gouverneur Morris questioned Yates.

Yates shrugged and feigned ignorance. He answered, "Susan is just a friend."

"And a friend of Captain Robert Drake, who hasn't been paying the right people for his business," Samuel Johnson told them.

"Who is there to pay besides the king?" Susan asked.

Samuel Johnson rolled his eyes in contempt. Gouverneur Morris leaned closer to the couple and said, "The captain hasn't been playing the game. He hasn't been paying the governor, who manages the troops, or the British soldiers, or those who own the governor, and much less those who oversee all these operations needed for colony security."

"I see," Susan replied, glancing down at the table.

"No, you don't," George Read continued. "We are accusing you of treason. We have a witness and a judge right here. Mr. Johnson, please declare court in session."

Yates fell over and collapsed on the floor. Susan rushed to help him. After checking his pulse and breath, she placed a fingertip in his tea and sniffed it.

"You've poisoned him!" she cried.

Yates gasped for air. Looking into her eyes, he asked, "Marry me."

Before she could respond, the manager of the site came over to the table. Accompanied by several waiters and one servant from Deborah Reed, he drew his sword and pointed it at the three legislators. The waiters drew their guns. He told the men, "I am charging the three of you with murder."

"On what evidence?" Samuel asked.

"We have several witnesses, a doctor, and a vial of poison with the Gouveneur's name on it."

"Where did you find that?" Gouveneur asked. Yates only has six minutes to live."

A chef took his sword and sliced the Gouveneur's leg. Quickly, he tied a cloth napkin as a tourniquet to avoid further blood loss. The other two men waved their white napkins in surrender.

"I have several demands," the manager persisted. "My name is Daniel Smith and I want the proprietorship of City Tavern. The tavern shall be treated as a new nation underneath the Eagles' proposed Bill of Rights. This means that the commerce of City Tavern will continue despite the war. We will conduct business with whom we wish, which presently includes English, French, Indians, and colonists."

Susan whispered to the young man dying in her arms, "Yates, we are legal. Our high flying ideals have returned to nest. Tell me who is behind you."

"Who paid you to do this?" Daniel Smith questioned the men, while the waiters carried Yates's body to the carriage outside.

"Catherine, the Czarina of Russia," George replied.

Daniel kept his sword aimed at the men as he spoke in private to Susan. "When did you and Yates become lovers?"

"Last week," she mentioned. "I turned fifteen."

Daniel motioned for the chef to replace him. Lowering his sword, he directed Susan to a small, hidden room behind the kitchen area. Susan entered through the secret door and discovered a room where the four walls and ceiling were completely covered in amber crystals.

He explained as he followed behind her. "Captain Drake spoke to me about the need to have City Tavern for the network. The Russian czarina is working with the M33 Arachnids and Gauds."

"Let me guess," Susan said as she strained her neck to study the ceiling. "They wanted a ritual murder for their portal and connection to their masters."

"Yes, I seized the room from Catherine," he said. "The Eagles can use the psychic protection of the amber crystals for the transport of souls."

Tears rolled down her eyes, and she hugged Daniel. "Yates is safe, despite the trauma."

"Yates is safe," he repeated. "Now hurry. I must release these men as part of the deal. You need a head start. Leave for Boston tonight with Joseph. I have already sent a messenger. Bury Yates at East Falls on the way out. He'll float down river, and his death will appear as a drowning. The truth will surface when appropriate. Our new nation is small and not ready for war."

"I suspect that Catherine used this room when she assassinated her husband, the czar," Susan commented. "I think that it should hold for the Eagles."

"There's more," Daniel said before summoning the cook to bring Greg. "Here's the baby for you and Yates. Time to bring young Greg out of the closet."

Unnerved, Susan turned around abruptly as several tears streaked down her face. "Where?"

"Here," he said. "We all heard Yates propose. The son of your friend Maria Theresa Gates must be kept secret. She is the British general's daughter. She was raped by the Sons of Liberty."

"The Sons of Liberty are spies for the British corporation." Susan reeled backwards and braced herself against the wall of the room. She held her abdomen and bowed her head to regain her composure.

"You can understand the corporate model."

"It is complicated. Yates brought in those such as Hancock and Adams, who will betray us to the East India Company. For these people, freedom is simply a matter of business. Yates served as the spokesperson for a brilliant woman, who understood the legal system far greater than anyone I've met so far. Her name is Elizabeth Carter," Susan told him as she handed over some papers that Yates gave her shortly before he died. She added, "This British poet works with the French, the ones covering Annapolis. Susan paused for a moment, before deciding firmly, "If Maria can deliver in secret, then I can raise my son without anyone's knowledge of his origins." Standing erect, she said, "It will be a good excuse to explain my absence for the past few months, and my need to hide for the next five months."

"The child will be in Boston. Nathan Hale can meet you there." Then he ushered her out of the room and on her way. "Don't worry, he'll find you."

Chapter Nineteen

Front lines are messy

----With permission from Alima

Reference Tune: *Send In the Clowns*

----Judy Collins

GRIEF-STRICKEN, JOSEPH and Susan somberly rode out of Philadelphia. They were accompanied by Franklin's love child with another woman. Benjamin Franklin admitted the existence of his son shortly before co-habiting with the first love of his life. Deborah Reed had raised William Franklin as if he was her own son and wished to protect him. Yate's murder meant that Deborah's relations might be targeted, and so they decided to take William to the cooperative in Lexington.

"Why does Catherine the Czarina want America for the Russian Empire?" Susan asked.

"You must understand the history of Russian money to answer that question," Joseph quipped.

"When Constantine took his empire to that part of the world, he abandoned his Roman legions. His serpentine generals became Jews to rise above the scramble for power. They coerced the sons of Abraham, who were already serpentine slaves on the Spice Route, to become their allies. Families such as the Bethmanns and Bauers became fierce rivals within the remaining Holy Roman Empire."

For a moment he paused as he directed Susan and horse toward a fork in the road.   Motioning her to take the right trail, he continued, "The Rothschilds recently stole the Bayer's coat of arms. After losing ground in the Seven Years War, they intended to use the Russian court to invade America as an important piece of the spice route."

"Is that another reason why Nathan and the others decided to call themselves Ducks? They are countering the purse strings of the Hebrew occultist named Goose."

"Yes," Joseph answered, adjusting himself in the saddle. "Catherine's maid of honor was the top French spy d'Eon. Though, he won the confidence of the czarina, he might have difficulty getting out of England now."

"The first Catherine of Russian was a runaway serf, a Hebrew of the Lark tribe," Susan observed. "I think that name refers to Jeremiah."

"They wove dark magic into their names to avoid detection," Joseph said. "The Bauers served as army intelligence for the Holy Roman Empire. Catherine the First was used by the army to intermarry with the Romanovs, the cousins of King Arthur in Siberia. They pulled the first Romanov out of a monastery for Russian rule. Nobody else wanted it because of the treachery in the court."

"I suspect that in another hundred years, the Romanovs will survive to work with the Eagles in overcoming the spice route invaders," Susan commented softly. "For now, it is just another cow chase in the dung of the lost Hebrew tribes, which have fallen under the serpentine illusion of freedom. Catherine the First served as a royal slave."

A rider stepped out of the shadows ahead. Waiting for them, John Andre sat mounted on a horse standing in the middle of the dirt road. Even in the dusk, Susan could recognize the familiar figure by the way he occupied the saddle.

"I overheard your discussion concerning the cow chase," John Andre said quietly. "It's great poetic material. The control of the spice route lies in Kochi, India, which means cow. Sometimes, we must chase what is sacred to us. I am a peacock like Freddy. Some of the royal progeny, legitimate or not, value freedom."

"John Andre," she gasped. "I thought that you were in Lexington with Eva. What brings you here?"

"You do," he said. "I am sorry about Yates. Sam Adams has gone into hiding as a result of the circumstances surrounding his death. You'll never find Sam without my help. He needs to see you and Joseph."

By passing the main thoroughfares of New York, the group obtained a carriage with the aid of the major and drove on to Boston. Three miles west of Faneuil Hall, they stopped at an inn. John Andre offered to take the horses and carriage. "Go on in. Sam has a room near the library."

In the library, they found Sam talking to a militia officer. After brief condolences, Sam introduced the man next to him. "Please meet John Parker. He is the head of the Lexington militia and will take William and Susan back safely to the cooperative."

Nabby Adams joined them in the library and they talked into the night. Later, John Andre escorted Susan to her room down the hall. He remarked, "So Daniel held the tavern hostage and the three legislators plea-bargained. Then there is the British-Prussia-Russia connection."

"What do you know about this connection?" Susan asked.

"Do you mind if we talk privately, perhaps in the study?" he questioned her.

Susan nodded and they briskly entered another room around the corner. Crossing her arms, she leaned against the desk and waited for John Andre to speak. He stepped in front of her to examine some nearby stacks.

"I was the one who warned Daniel Smith," he began. "Catherine the Czarina thought that she could teleport Russian troops on the continent after the Seven Years War. The Russians like their jeweled ornaments, and have a major stake in world trade."

"It is quite a contrast to the Puritans who fled the conflicts wrought by greed," Susan commented.

"It is enough to keep us all simply fashioned," he commented. After a sigh, he turned toward Susan, "There is a world conflict between over-indulgence and simplicity. Those who endured the hardship of bringing the Glastonbury project to the new world intend to keep their purified ways."

"I sense that you had a revelation in Germany," Susan told him. Turning away from him, she elaborated. "After the death of the captain's child, Eva and I looked for a new home. I found one with Mrs. Reed, Yates, Joseph, Nathan, and the others. Meanwhile, you take care of Eva without her being aware of it."

"Yes, I am Eva's admirer," he said. Shifting his stance from one foot to the other, John Andre changed the subject and persisted with his explanation. "They created the Amber Room in 1716 and used it to tie allies together in masked persecution of the Avalon and Glastonbury descendants. They are not uniting against Switzerland. They intend to destroy any refugee with a connection to benevolent extraterrestrials. People forget that the descendants of Jesse, the light spirit that they crucified in the Israeli insurrection, fled to Georgia, Russia, rather than the Georgia south of New England. Britain hopes to create a new world order with New England, an enterprise intending to finish the job of extinguishing the world's Light."

"In the meantime, they invoke their intergalactic aliens for help," Susan commented.

"Yes, the Eagles are really the Italian Black knights from the ancient kingdom of Camelon," Andre continued. "The Avalon refugees in Switzerland are the descendants of the Pink knights. Noah's ark docked in the Swiss Alps after the major flood. A Roman emperor in Turkey intends to relocate the ark to his turf to fool history. The descendants of Enoch from Noah's time are the ones Britain pursued in Germany. Those in Sweden that the Prussian-Russian alliance intends to destroy are descended from the first Dragon flyers. Like some of those in Africa."

"You must have recognized this in the West Indies," Susan said.

"Yes, Deborah Reed's first husband went into hiding due to his vulnerability as a merchant. William Franklin is a target for similar reasons."

"So what do we do now?" Susan questioned him. "They are trying to kill me to get to the captain. The Eagles have a lot more work to do."

"Go back to Lexington with Parker and William. Continue drilling with the militia. Teach Parker how to remotely access the Amber Room through the seized portal at City Tavern."

"But Parker only protects the wealthy men, who trade with the East India Company," Susan reminded Andre. "He leads the militia because he doesn't have long to live."

Andre blinked. "Correct. Parker serves as the company patriots weak link. Use this to your advantage," he insisted. "Parker will not refuse you, because his heart knows the truth behind the compromised people who commissioned him."

Susan and the others departed early the next morning, leaving John Andre with the Adams relations. They beat off all threats and made quick time to the cooperative in Lexington. After their arrival, Susan began reviewing the alien papers that Nabby had given her before they left. Eva divided her time between the shop and the homestead that she and Daniel were constructing in Concord.

Shortly after their return, Nathan Hale brought a classmate from Yale.

"Meet Benjamin Tallmadge," Nathan said. "We plan to work as instructors after college. I graduate next week."

"I must be back soon," Tallmadge said. "My fraternity is conducting a special meeting."

"Which frat?" Nathan asked. "I didn't know that you were in a secret organization."

"The Liona," he replied with a shrug. "Speaking of organizations, what is Boone doing with the Watauga Association in North Carolina?"

"I'm not sure," Susan answered. "It might have something to do with Culper's Ring in New York."

"Hmm, I'll have to talk to Boone sometime. He may be infringing on our operation," Tallmadge said, ruefully rubbing his head.

Meanwhile, Susan continued drilling with Parker's minute forces, and Parker developed the skill of remotely accessing portals for protection. Upset about the ambush at City Tavern, Freddy retreated to John Andre's home in Lexington approximately four miles away. Unlike the local schools, the academy continued to shelter the children from the surrounding world issues. Freddy quit drilling with the militia to focus on his studies.

John Andre arrived two weeks later. After checking in on Freddy, he arrived at the Buckham Tavern at a time he knew it would be emptied of customers.

Susan greeted him as he took a seat at the counter. "What brings you here? Freddy? Eva?"

"I have started to wonder whether Freddy is getting the proper education for his eventual princely duties. Seems that you and some of the others may be better prepared for what life brings you."

"As long as we don't lose our lives getting the education," Susan remarked as she brought over a bowl of stew and cup of herb tea. "Freddy is concerned that the Eagles might fight against his country. So are the wife and daughter of General Gage."

"It must have been quite the opportunity to browse through Franklin's library," Andre commented, sipping his tea slowly.

"If I had been an adult male, I would have been seen as a competitor. If it wasn't for Yates and Joseph, I might have appeared as one of Franklin's mistresses. Falling in love with Yates made me less of a threat to Deborah Reed and provided cover as a beau rather than a serious student."

"The legislative elite are threatened by young enquirers, particularly the female mind," he said.

"If Yates had survived the inquiry, and we had married, I am not sure if the proposed documents would have ever been undertaken in the same manner," Susan reflected. "I am busy gathering the research needed for a declaration of independence and constitution. Boone is piloting some of the finer points in his Watauga Association."

"Do you mean his fledging republic near North Carolina?" Andre asked.

"It is the most independent area on the map," she said. "I don't think it will last long."

"Why?" he questioned.

"Like the plantation owners around him, Boone is more interested in building his own empire," Susan said. She looked down at the counter and rubbed out a spot. "I think he is using Eva to get his hands on the sunstone necklace. It won't work for him."

"Theft is different from an inherited heirloom and tradition infused with the power of love," he commented. Then he added, "The former school instructor with the other half of the necklace is indirectly working for Sam Adams."

"That is the nature of the sunstone crystal," Susan said. "The thieves start working for us. Its mission cannot be stolen."

Andre laughed. His hand swirled the tea around in his cup as he spoke. "Is that why Eva broke off the engagement?"

"She is still in the relationship, but pretending to be fickle-hearted," Susan said. "He won't leave because he covets what we are doing here."

"What are we doing here?" he asked with a smirk, staring into her eyes.

"After spending a year with you on a ship, I know better than to get lost in your rhetoric. John Andre, what book are you reading now?"

John Andre pulled a small booklet from his pocket. Dangling it between himself and Susan, he began thumbing through it. Susan seized it from him and walked away from the counter before he could protest.

She said, "I need to read whatever is on your mind, so I can stay two steps ahead of you. I know why all the women love you. It is because you educate them."

"Is that what attracted you to Yates?" he asked.

"No, I was already schooled in the ways of government," she said. "What attracted me was the fact that he still believed in a political system. His visionary sense of order shone like a beacon in these chaotic times. It just is that I would have had to do all the work. He kept me on track, though."

"And Boone?" he asked.

"He is just a plow in the field where we sow the seeds of freedom," Susan said, slumping over the counter and leaning on her elbows. "See, both Freddy and Eva have already accused me of sounding as philosophical as you."

Hearing herself, she stared into his eyes. "The problem is that you are on the other side."

"Not quite. I am mending my ways after Germany and the Boston Massacre," he said. "I have a mission for you and Freddy. You owe me for getting you out of City Tavern."

"What is it?"

"One of the men, who the British shot, was a runaway from Michie Tavern. His name was Crispus Attucks, and his son Estabrook escaped to City Tavern. He'll be safer here."

"You want Freddy and me to go to City Tavern to cover for Estabrook?"

"He intends to join the Lexington minute forces."

"Michie Tavern is in the heart of Jacobite country," Susan mentioned.

"Thomas Jefferson will help you. Not the plantation owner on the mountain, but the African captive that bears his name. He wants to escape, too, and Estabrook can help."

"Could he lift some of Jefferson's books? Maybe permanently borrow them until we're done with legalities?" Susan asked. "Sounds like a deal."

Chapter Twenty

Some fires are hard to put out

Reference Tune: *Burn*

----Ellie Goulding

"I UNDERSTAND THAT the Michie Tavern serves women, which differs from the new policy at City Tavern," Susan continued.

"You've made an impression," John Andre quipped. Then he added, "Daniel wishes to avoid complications. The only people in the assemblies are men. He doesn't want any distractions for his displaced Englishmen support group. It is sort of a consciousness-raising. These guys are behind the times."

"So we free up their slaves and books, then serve it to them in a different dish."

"As I said, we don't want complications," Andre reminded her. "We have to keep it serious, and make them think that a new nation is their own idea."

"They can run interference between us and the British and all the others who want a piece of the American pie."

"There's another matter concerning the stolen necklace," he said. "The Tories are intending to dump tea in Boston Harbor, and blame it on the patriots."

"There is no such thing as a patriot on this continent," Susan answered. "If this was true, the British would arrest Knox and his militia in

Boston Commons. Instead they harass the Lexington and Acton forces, so we must conduct covert drills."

"Yes, Isaiah Thomas's publication Massachusetts Spy fools no one. No real spy would print their work in black in white. It is like the Junius Letters. Probably the same people behind the annoyance."

"Do you think Isaiah Thomas is working with John Wilkes?" Susan asked.

"Yes, but that is the least of our worries," he told her.

"Why doesn't Sam tell them to shuck the oysters at Union Oyster House instead? The fish would feel better," Susan said.

"Governor Hutchinson would prefer that. The Union Oyster House spouts the Massachusetts Spy with its menu," John Andre observed. He sighed. "Dumping tea makes more of a statement concerning British culture. It is not about the bankrupt corporate ships. It is more about who is king of the harbor."

"Keep me out of it," Susan said. "My mission here is to keep Buckham Tavern open."

Susan and John Andre quieted when Eva suddenly emerged from the kitchen. Almost slamming some heavy pots down on the counter, she blurted, "Benjamin Rush and the Sons of Liberty are going to ruin everything."

Andre glanced at Susan before he spoke. He softly asked Eva with a slight smile, "Have you been spying on us?"

Eva wiped her brow and wiped her hands on her apron. "Only part of the time."

"Did you overhear us talking about you?" Susan asked.

"Were you talking about me?"

"No, never," John Andre said, leaning back in his chair. "What do you know about Dr. Rush?"

"Don't believe John Andre," Susan said.

"I don't," Eva said before addressing his question.

"It is what happens when you spy," John Andre told her. "Now what do you know about the Sons of Liberty?"

"They take liberties with anyone who crosses them," she said.

"Just what I suspected," John Andre said as he rubbed his chin. "We must not interfere with them.

Chapter Twenty-One

Those who are trapped in their own illusion scream loudest

Reference Tune: *Meet Virginia*

----Train

IN MARCH OF 1773, Freddy, Susan, and Joseph Adams went to Williamsburg, Virginia, for a meeting at the House of Burgess. Sam Adams had reported on the Eagle's Bill of Rights last November. Delegates from many of the wealthy plantations in Jacobite territory suddenly wanted to develop their own shadow government, complete with the Eagle's Bill of Rights. After her discussion with Eva and John Andre on the Sons of Liberty, Susan raised doubts about Virginia's sincerity.

Unlike the assemblies in Pennsylvania, often termed the city of brotherly love, the houses in Virginia enjoyed the company of both genders. Susan took a seat at the far right of the House of Burgess and watched the proceedings. Many of the Charlottesville plantation owners wanted to adopt the notion of individual rights because it had become trendy, especially at parties. Somewhat influenced by the legal practice of John Adams, delegates from the Williamsburg area savored the notion of education and human rights.

A representative by the name of Patrick Henry made the pitch for a standing committee to network with the Massachusetts Committee of Correspondence. The delegates seemed almost bored with the proceedings.

People became impatient and demanded an early break. Some wanted to spend their time catching up on local news and gossip. Others wanted to meet the young Duke of York and invite him to formalities. While the others split off into various cliques, Susan wandered into the garden during recess. Rushing outside to compose himself, Patrick Henry followed Susan into the yard. For a few moments, she stood admiring the flowery array and aromas. Patrick blocked her way along one of the garden paths. She turned her head, rather than confront him directly.

"Give me liberty or give me death!" she yelled at him.

He backed off with a grin, standing aside so that Susan would be free to pass.

"I'm glad someone was paying attention," he told her.

"You're gonna have to speak louder," she told him. "Make it sound like a party or something. You're different from Jefferson, Monroe, and Madison."

"They all come from some hill in Charlottesville," he said. "The Williamsburg scene doesn't want to give up any luxuries.

"If these wealthy plantation owners have any more liberties, the tavern owners will be penniless. They intend to drive free trade out of business. They already have their connections established with the machinations of the Crown."

"Except it is a different Crown than George's," Patrick said.

"That is what happens when your educational establishments are called William and Mary," Susan added. "The transfer of the Crowns is sometimes just a sleight of hand."

A familiar figure joined their discussion in the garden. He seemingly appeared out of nowhere. His manner was calm and pleasant compared to the boisterous chatter around them.

"Hello, John Andre," Susan greeted. "Come join me for Patrick's next inspiring speech. I want to have a good time."

Patrick laughed. "I'll be pulling the war over their eyes."

"So to speak," Susan said. "Make it a party. It is the only way you'll get your point across. None of the people here have martyr potential. Their passions are for over-consumption."

"They won't hear me until the cannon ball goes flying over their roof," Patrick mentioned.

"No, this is not the warrior class," Andre said, escorting Susan to the next session. "War for them is merely paperwork. They have no concept of what a true revolution would require."

"Some will be unpleasantly surprised," Patrick reflected.

By the end of the next session, Freddy came racing toward them. Before they had a chance to take a break with the others, Freddy stood in the aisle in front of them. He was breathing heavily and beads of sweat dripped from his brow.

"Let's get out of here," he said. "Susan, I've talked Thomas Jefferson into letting us tour his library."

Which Thomas Jefferson?" John Andre asked.

"The dark-haired sage that lives at Monticello," Freddy said. "The red-haired, noble socialite of Williamsburg is called T.J. to avoid confusion. Both are astute politicians."

"T.J. has the bigger heart, like the rest of John Adams's crowd," Susan added as she headed for the door. Buzzing past Freddy, she changed the subject, "Great idea, Prince. I want to leave before they start asking about Yeats and questioning our ideas."

"No, this is not the proper forum for those kinds of discussions," John Andre softly said, hurrying to catch up with Susan.

Susan stopped short and stared at him. "You know, John Andre, you are a nice friend."

"I'll meet you back at the Lexington cooperative," he said. "I have business in New York that requires my attention, especially now that I understand what is happening here."

Susan and Freddy easily convinced Joseph Adams to leave Williamsburg for Monticello. They journeyed by carriage and found the home site empty, except for the slave town around the building. They wandered through the grounds, looking for a dark-skinned man named Thomas Jefferson.

After a half hour, a man in his late teens appeared from one of the huts alongside the dirt road. "My name is Tom Jefferson."

"Can you lead us to Mr. Jefferson's library?" Joseph Adams asked him.

He took them inside the main house and into a large bedroom. Shelves of books and artifacts lined some of the walls in the north corner.

"If you are looking for reading material on governing bodies, I suggest these," Tom said as he pulled a few off the shelves. "There's a few on politics and philosophies concerning ancient Greece."

"Great, just what we need," Susan said, stashing a few in a sack. "We'll leave a note, letting Thomas know that I've borrowed them until October. If he wants his books back, he'll have to make the colonist's meeting in Philadelphia."

"Want to come along too?" Freddy questioned Tom. "We'll put it in the note that the prince required the services of a Tom Jefferson."

Tom's eyes lit up with Freddy's proposal. "I can help you with your work. Mr. Jefferson inadvertently taught me everything he knows."

"Good deal, Tom," Susan said. She bounced impatiently on her toes. "Let's get over to Michie Tavern before the overseers notice that you are missing. We'll put it all in the letter, but I doubt that the others know how to read."

Freddy went with Tom to help him pack while Susan and Joseph checked out a few more books. They met at the bottom of the hill, where they hid Tom inside the carriage next to Susan. Then they drove several miles to a tavern on a stagecoach run. They were met on the road by Mrs. Michie.

"Hurray inside, while the mister is out hunting with the boys. Park out back. I have a few more African captives to deliver. These came from the royal family in Cameroon."

"We won't stay long," Susan told her. "Thank you so much for your hospitality."

"My pleasure," Mrs. Michie replied. "In a couple of years, we'll probably be in a revolution. The time to convince Virginia to join on the side of freedom is now."

Tom helped the royal family from Cameroon store their things inside a wagon near the parked carriage. They unloaded the carriage, while Susan, Freddy, and Joseph enjoyed a brief meal. Moments later, they slipped out of the tavern before the arrival of the next scheduled coach. Reaching Lexington at the end of April, they found another coach for the African family and sent them to City Tavern with William Franklin. Freddy left for England the next day.

"You must have heard the latest news," John Andre told Susan when he came to take Freddy. "Patrick Henry roused the delegates in Virginia. The only problem is that they are blaming their lack of freedom on Freddy's father." He playfully swung the eleven-year-old boy to his shoulder before adding, "We are getting Freddy out of the country just in time. By the way, Mrs. Patrick Henry requested that I give you this note."

Susan opened the sweet-smelling envelope and read the writing on elegant stationary.

To the proprietress of Buckham Tavern
Please escort Mr. Patrick Henry to the October meeting
In Philadelphia
We appreciated your help in Virginia
Thank you again for your
Wonderful hospitality
----Sara

"Is the wife of Patrick Henry ill?" Susan asked John Andre.

"She has another life as a spy for the colonists," he reported. "Patrick is being targeted for his leadership in Virginia. People say she is in confinement, but she really does her best to avoid the Jacobites as well as the Hanover kingdom. It is why he is so ardent now."

"Does she intend to use Hanover Tavern as another stop on the freedom underground?" Susan asked.

"Yes, she wants you to cover for Mr. Henry. She admires your single-minded purpose," Andre told her. "Mrs. Henry will start passing along African captives shortly after the Philadelphia meeting."

"The gentry of Virginia certainly have different social mores from those in Pennsylvania," Susan observed.

"Yes, liberty is becoming respectable, and so is the life of loved ones," John Andre said.

"Apparently, we are all in this together," Susan said. "She knows that we like each other."

"Apparently," he echoed. "There is no turning back now. She is not waiting for a response," he said. "She made an assumption that Patrick will be passing through shortly after the summer. If you reject him, he may not make it to Philadelphia alive."

Chapter Twenty-Two

Appreciate all that meanders

Reference Tune: *Slow Ride*

----Foghat

BY THE TIME Patrick Henry journeyed to Buckham Tavern, Lieutenant Governor Hutchison had published a series of letters arguing for 'respectful liberties.' When Susan and Patrick arrived in Philadelphia together, they stayed in a cabin on the outskirts of town. The cabin stood on a bluff overlooking the waterfront where the captain's ship, the Camden, was anchored. Less than a half mile away was an Iroquois Indian camp, which offered protection in case Susan and Patrick needed to flee for safety. Her dealings through agents such as Boone and Gibson had prepared the way for their meeting in conjunction with the colonial convention. Names and whereabouts were held securely because nobody knew which way the winds of war would blow. The undeclared revolution compelled the Lexington cooperative to adopt desperate measures.

On the first night of their arrival, Susan ventured to the Iroquois campfire, while Patrick renewed his acquaintance with the city. He wanted to meet delegations from the other colonies as well as check in with his colleagues from Virginia. Since the formation of Virginia's Committee of Correspondence, many other states followed with their own. The fork in the road had been taken, and now they wanted to use their combined power to promote an economy independent from England. The first order of business involved the repeal of the Tea Act, which attempted to give the United India Company a monopoly.

After parting ways in the late afternoon, Susan walked toward the edge of the bluff for a better view of her surroundings. Despite the tension in the air, she became immediately aware of the bounty surrounding her. Osprey, eagles, heron, crows, hawks, and gulls soared high in the sky overhead. Fruit trees and berry bushes around her were filled with ripe fruit for picking. From her bird's-eye perspective on the cliff, she could see the dinghies fully packed with mussels, clams, oysters, cod, and salmon. Hawkers at the water's edge hawked a variety of produce and rich textiles. The eyes of the feathered creatures flying above her seemed fixated on the seafood below. They flew in spirals around the wharf, and occasionally made a kill of their own with a swooping dive.

An Iroquois man joined her at the bluff. Studying the view from her perspective, he swiftly cast a sideways glance at her when he found the words to begin. His tone came from the heart like an arrow piercing the air between them. He confided, "The Seven Years War destroyed our peaceful league of nations."

"I know," Susan said softly, staring down the bluff.

"A revolution would obliterate us," he said.

"I know," she repeated. "I want to learn from your confederacy. I want to know how you were able to create peace between five different nations. I also want to know where it went wrong." Facing him, she explained, "The existence of a peaceful confederacy must be immune from the international powers of conquest and exploitation."

His fierce countenance softened, and he told her, "Come to our fire tonight, where you can observe how we govern. The women serve as arbitrators. They interpret the laws with their courts or purposeful gatherings. The leaders of the tribes execute their decisions, unless they or representatives disagree or have questions. We work it out. All is done in harmony with the natural world."

Susan took a deep breath of the autumn air, and quietly followed the man to the campfire. Before she sat down in the circle of people congregated around the fire, he pointed to a large, ancient bird watching the group. The creature remained in the tree, and reflected the demeanor of the chiefs placidly sitting below.

"Look," he told Susan. "We are being guided by the spirit of the great blue heron. It is not a bird of war or peace."

"It stands on its own," one of the wise women interjected. "The blue heron makes a stand for self-sufficiency, preferring to determine its own destiny."

Susan quietly listened as the others told her about the totem.

"Its power is in its legs, and the ability to wade in the depths of consciousness."

"They don't form colonies. Their associations are limited to a few birds at a time."

After hearing their words, Susan commented, "The blue heron finds opportunity, and makes the most of it."

"Yes," another woman elder said. "Fly with the eagles, but be a blue heron."

A chief sitting near her reached for the necklace around her neck. Holding it in his palm, he offered it back to her with a comment, "Your heart power is in this necklace. It is time to regroup in order to soar to your destiny."

"Those who gave it to me are dead. I have been living on borrowed time," she said. "The gift of life came with the necklace."

"That time is done," he told her. "Time to find other loves and live again."

Susan stayed for several hours at the campfire, and listened to their songs and stories. When the moon disappeared behind some tall pines, she rose and left. The Iroquois brave walked with her until they were within fifty yards of the cabin. Smoke from the chimney and a candle in the window informed them that Patrick had already returned from town. After a brief farewell, Susan knocked on the door of the cabin and entered. She found Patrick sitting in a rocking chair by the fire. Immediately he went to the door to bolt it behind her. Then he blew out the candle and scattered the wood in the fire so that it would scarcely burn.

Susan took off her garments and went to bed. Patrick joined her. Placing his bare arm around her, he drew her to him. His warmth comforted her.

"It must not have gone very well," she observed.

"Yes, I'm scared," he commented. "These colonists don't know what they are talking about."

"I'm scared too," she told him. "The Iroquois do know what they are talking about."

"Tell me more. I am in need of their wisdom."

"The spirit of the Blue Heron guided the camp counsel. "It wasn't a cougar, bear, or otter. It was a bird. Birds represent consciousness."

"That's not good," Patrick said. "This means that we are dealing with inspiration rather than embodiment."

"Yes, we must wade in the waters of spirit for sustenance," Susan added. "Though we may not become a tangible presence, we must hold the position in the realms of thought and consciousness."

"We have more work to do. We must support our position legally."

"I agree. The Iroquois Confederacy did not have any support in the legal world, which served as the foothold for the Roman conquerors left behind in Europe."

"Tomorrow, I'll get you into the Philosophical Society and the library. People asked about my wife," he said. "They know that a doctor said that she suffered from mental illness and doesn't get out. They don't know that the diagnosis is a cover for her work with the Freedom Trail."

"Some people will recognize me from the tavern," Susan said.

"They see you as a curious hostess. Those at this convention fear your charms," he said. "It's their fault that they don't take women seriously and treat them as well as the Iroquois. Please, don't threaten them or erase their delusion, yet," he said. "They are in for enough of a culture shock as it is."

"And play our cards carefully, so we don't lose it all," Susan remarked. "My enemies are only being held in check."

"There is more than our lives at stake here," he added.

"Perhaps the world of humanity is at risk as well," she said before drifting into a light sleep.

The next day, Susan accompanied Patrick to a social gathering at the Philosophical Society. While the colonists conversed, Susan wandered into the library section and perused the stacks of books. After slipping a few chosen volumes in a sack tucked underneath her shawl, she went outside for some fresh air. Susan found their carriage parked a few blocks away, and exchanged the sack of books for an empty one.

Walking toward the governmental library near Carpenter Hall, she met Patrick halfway down the mall.

"There you are," he greeted as he locked his arm inside hers. "Let's go check out the next library. I have some legal work to do, and need your assistance. I understand the origins of the captain and how a protégé of Lord Russell stole the family name. But, there is one thing both you and the captain overlooked."

"What is that?" she asked as they walked inside the building together.

"The Spencers also suffered similar treatment," he told her. "After Walpole and his parliamentary machines succeeded in orphaning Lady Diana Spencer, the Russell family arranged to marry her. Her father had been the first lord of the treasury before Walpole. A relation of the captain's family provided a dowry for her marriage to the Prince of Wales, but Walpole blocked it."

"Why?" Susan questioned after they stepped inside the government library.

"The Spencers are descendants of King Arthur's half-brother Dadgon. Dadgon was the son of King Arcas and Queen Eilene, the Green Knight who reigned the United Kingdom after the Turks destroyed Camelon. The captain's ancestors were also Green knights."

"The first success at settling this terrain was achieved by the Pilgrim Spencers. Like the Drake Family, they served as earls for many kings."

"There's more to the story," Patrick told her. "Robin Hood's Maid Miriam was a Spencer in Eleanor's Court."

"Let me guess, Mr. Henry," Susan said while eyeing the collection. "An English king stole your father's family name."

Susan waited for his reply as she straightened the shelves. The books that she wanted projected several inches further than the others.

"Correct," Patrick said retrieving the books that she chose.

After she left to fetch some cups of coffee, Patrick removed them from the shelves and placed them on a desk. Susan returned with the beverages. After placing the saucers on the table, she began packing her bag sitting in a chair below the table. Patrick put a few books in his pocket, and they quickly left the room together. While Patrick stayed and attended meetings, Susan visited Deborah Reed at Franklin Court.

"Looks like you are over Yates," Deborah observed when the attendant deposited the bags of books on the doorstep.

Susan waved the carriage off, and responded, "He would be happy about the latest acquisitions and developments."

Susan, Benny, and Deborah studied the texts as they discussed their next move. Susan told them about the blue heron and the Iroquois system of government. She also talked about her experiences in Virginia.

"What we need now is a flag," Deborah said.

"A Blue Heron flag!" Benny exclaimed with delight.

"Yes, I'll have the ladies help me with the project right away. Meanwhile, you can go over the material as we sew. We'll make as many as we can."

Within minutes, five other women from Deborah's sewing circle arrived and drew up a design in the parlor. The women had been awaiting Deborah's signal for action, no matter what it entailed. They brightened and expressed relief at the relatively easy assignment. Susan continued to peruse books from the library and presented the material as the collective worked on the flag. Patrick visited them later in the evening, and expressed appreciation for their progress.

"We are finally getting somewhere," he told them as he eyed the design. Then he addressed Susan quietly in the adjacent hall, "Spend the night at Franklin Court. It will confuse those who have been watching us."

Deborah overheard and nodded in agreement. "The colonists are really upset about the additional tax. Infiltrators are already manipulating the hysteria."

"What have you heard?" Patrick asked.

Deborah turned her head in the direction of the women busy in the parlor. "My sources tell me that the owner of the Codhouse Tavern in Lincoln, Massachusetts is operating a spy ring at Yale."

Patrick glanced outside a window. Susan looked in the direction of his focus, and saw the captain tapping on the pane.

"There's my signal," he said before rushing out the door. "I'll check-in tomorrow."

The following day, Patrick did not return until late in the evening. This time he dashed inside when Deborah opened the door. Without wasting time in explanations, he grabbed Susan's arms and faced her. "We must flee to Boston. The captain's horses are waiting outside the window."

Deborah quickly gathered the completed flag and thrust it into Susan's hands. "We have two extras. Hurry out the window as I hand you your things."

They galloped to the captain's ship and rode the horses straight up the incline. Various crew members took the horses to the hold after Susan and Patrick dismounted. The mates hurriedly untied the ship from the dock, and sailed it from the harbor. Susan and Patrick found the captain sitting inside his quarters.

"Looks like we have some time to catch up," he told them. "Great to see you again, even if it is under duress."

"Did you get a chance to learn more about the Codhouse?" Patrick questioned Susan.

"Yes, the owner has relations to Lord Russell in England as well as the benefactors, who pirated the captain's last name."

"Drake?" Patrick questioned. "How far away is Codhouse from the Lexington cooperative?"

"It is right next door. They cut off some of Lexington to make it," she answered.

"Maybe we can get Dr. Joseph Adams to relocate, and keep an eye on the place," the captain remarked.

"Do you think the Codhouse has something to do with why we needed to leave tonight?" Susan asked.

"The king's tax collectors were killed by the colonists," Patrick said. "They are willing to murder tea agents to avoid taxes."

"Some of the colonists behave like pirates, because they are pirates," Susan stated.

Think about it," The captain said. "There's Jacobites as well as William and Mary in Patrick's Virginia, corporate Elizabethans in parts of Massachusetts, Penn and Pitt in Pennsylvania, and George's soldiers all over the place. We must avoid a royal war in the colonies."

"So what are we?" Patrick asked. "If we call ourselves Eagles, we infuriate all of them. Demonic pirates directly compete with the spiritual knights protecting the Spice Route."

"Blue Herons," Susan announced, unfurling one of the flags. "Raise your flag, captain."

Chapter Twenty-Three

Until someone is in the clear

It is difficult to know

What has brought them

To their eventual destination

Reference Tune: *A Horse With No Name*

----America

THEY ARRIVED IN Boston Harbor just ahead of three British ships, which Parliament had sent to protect the Tea Act. Though officials denied prior knowledge of the murder of the tea agents in Philadelphia, the timing of the enforcers appeared more than coincidental. Dr. Joseph Warren, an activist with the Boston Committee of Correspondence, sponsored an article in the Massachusetts Spy. The Boston Committee of Correspondence differed immensely from the state committee established by Sam Adams. Patriot pirates controlled the city committee.

The newspaper version of the Philadelphia incident contrasted greatly with the experiences of those raising the flag of the Blue Heron. The publisher, Isaiah Thomas, claimed that Boston endorsed the eviction of the tea agents in Philadelphia. Despite the presence of the three British ships in the harbor, Sons of Liberty pushed for the disposal of the tea agents in Boston. Meanwhile, Patrick Henry galloped home to Virginia, while the Eagles regrouped in the wine cellar at Green Dragon Tavern. Eva,

Captain Davis, John Parker, and Susan attended. The transformation of the Eagles' totem into a Blue Heron provided sufficient cover for the time being. The British soldiers and pirating patriots were watching for a different archetype in the lofty skies, while the Blue Herons stayed closer to earth.

After reading through the article at the meeting, the captain put the newspaper down on the center table. He told the Blue Herons present at the emergency gathering, "We are going to need two documents stating our position with the British Empire. One document will list the colonists' grievances and blame the situation on King George. We'll call document one The Declaration of Independence. Document two will be named The Declaration of Interdependence. In the second document, we'll acknowledge the parent countries, but let them know that we have left the nest and are out on our own. In this way, we distinguish ourselves from the evolving confusion and mayhem."

One member commented, "There's no forgiveness for the prodigal child this time. The violence is intolerable, especially those intent on keeping the nest clean."

"We can't live this way," another added. "We'll need to define ourselves regardless of parental support."

Further discussion was interrupted by the appearance of young Nathan Hale climbing down the cellar ladder. Still hanging onto the last few rungs, he told them, "The patriots are planning an attack on the East India Company ships in the harbor. They want to disguise themselves as Native Americans, and put on war paint."

"Seems rather childish to me," the captain interjected. "What does Sam Adams say about this?"

"Sam is still looking for a peaceful route out of Philadelphia. Nobody has told him yet," Nathan replied.

Captain Davis observed, "The three British ships will probably just sit back and watch the ruse. Maybe even help them dump parliamentary tea in the harbor."

"Those poor fish," Susan said. "Why couldn't they just stick with oysters?"

"It's against their religion," John Parker stated with a straight face.

"What do you mean? They aren't catholic," the captain said.

"No, but the company banks with the Vatican," Eva mentioned.

"It beats the king's purse strings in Kochi, India," Susan stated. Then she addressed the captain, "I think that it is time to get the Camden and the others out of Boston Harbor, while the rest of us throw a party in Lexington. I want a party that honors scarce world resources."

"Beer on the house?" John Parker questioned.

"For a night," Eva told him.

"We'll tell the Native Americans to clear the area," Captain Davis said. "They don't need to take the blame for this savage behavior."

Everyone quickly left the wine cellar to pursue their various missions. Susan and Nathan Hale were the last to leave the cellar. They lingered several minutes after the last Blue Heron exited the trapdoor at the top of the stairs.

"What do you get on Dr. Ben Rush?" Susan asked him. "Eva hasn't been pleased with his two-faced tactics on the underground freedom trail."

"Don't tell him about the work of the Blue Herons," Nathan replied. "He is in league with Dr. Warren and some of the other physicians with English connections. Though he has been great at helping Africans escape to freedom, he considers George Washington a heretic."

"Is George Washington a heretic?" Susan asked.

"He is untrustworthy," Nathan replied. "He will only free his slaves to soothe a guilty conscience after having beaten them so unmercifully. People like that can't be trusted. Dr. Rush sees through it, though he practices sanctioned medical violence. He and his colleagues poisoned the Native Americans during the Seven Years War. They poisoned the well at the Lexington schoolhouse. They purposely misuse bloodletting to carry out the mandates of the Sons of Liberty."

"Sounds diabolical," Susan commented.

"It is," he said. "Occultists of the Roman Empire have infiltrated the practice of medicine in England."

Susan turned and began climbing her way to the top. Nathan stood back and watched her. Wrinkling his brow, he told her, "I have more advice to offer."

She stopped on a rung and looked down at him. "What is it, Nathan?"

"Divide the Declaration of Interpendence into two halves and hide them."

Susan stared at him without saying another word.

He swallowed hard, and said, "John Hancock arrived here with the others tonight. He knows better, but his loyalty is to Parliament."

Susan slowly began her ascent. Without turning around, she said, "Tell Sam Adams to maintain a low profile for now."

When Susan poked her head through the trap door, she noticed an eerie green light pouring through the windows of a vacant tavern. Two familiar faces appeared from the shadows behind her. Eva stepped toward her as John Parker grabbed her upper arm.

"Alien attack," he whispered in the darkness. "Our best fight is on the Camden."

Eva motioned Nathan away from the light as he surfaced from the cellar below. He immediately ran for cover outside of the tavern as Susan consulted the sunstone necklace. A bright light shot from the crystal and protected Nathan as he ran down the opposite end of the street. They followed him out of the tavern and watched him mount his horse, which had been tied to a nearby grove of trees. Steadying himself in the saddle, he reined the horse around and galloped down a forest trail.

The threesome raced for the ship docked in the harbor. The light from the crystal continued to shelter them from the powerful laser beams of the alien ship. The mates had already opened fire on the spaceship, while other crew members raised the sails to catch the winds roaring through the wharves. The ship slowly began to move for safer waters as the alien ship sunk the British ships, Hancock's merchant ships, and the East India company ships. The other ships accompanying the Camden loomed ahead in the distant black horizon.

On board the Camden, Susan almost tripped over the legs of a dead alien lying next to the plank. The captain pulled her away from the sight and directed the rest to the far end of the boat. Eva tugged on John's sleeve, urging him away from the scene.

"They jumped our ship once they landed," the captain explained as he ran with them. "These Grays have been here since the days of King Arthur."

Susan slumped on the ship's floor when she reached the far end. Bending her knees toward her, she sobbed in the folds of her skirt. Flashing lights of various hues and winds from many different directions soared above her head. Eva remained in a huddle with John Parker beneath a wooden rail fifteen feet away. As the ship picked up speed and the winds coalesced into a strong, single breeze, Susan dried her tears and rose from her place. She stared into the silent distance as the salty air permeated her being.

"Nothing like the sight of a dead soul to age a person," Marcus told her as he joined her at the ship's edge.

"That's what the Grays are all about," she remarked.

"Ay-ay," he said with a nod. "The salt air takes away the horror, but it does nothing to relieve the hollow fright of the immortal souls that are black. If they don't scare you, the serpentine vampires will suck the life right out."

"Why didn't anyone notice their presence before they descended from the skies?" Susan asked.

"They've been hiding in another dimension," he said. "Things sunk so low when the Priory of Scion arrived that they came forward. They came with the three British ships. The soldiers didn't realize that some of the passengers were imposters."

Susan brightened with Marcus's explanation. She pointed at a body of land ahead. "It looks like the captain is stopping at the island over there."

"He wants to drop the three of you off," Marcus said. "I need to catch up with my frigate."

With his arm wrapped tightly around Eva, John approached them. He embraced Susan with his free arm as he remarked, "Here's our stop. We can hop a dinghy to the island and make our escape in the morning. Tonight we'll have a bonfire for the dead aliens."

"We don't want to be held responsible," Marcus stated.

"Looks like the aliens beat the patriots to their own tea party," Susan commented. For a moment, she left John's hold. Standing on her toes, she planted a soft kiss on Marcus's forehead. "Thank you for staying on the ship. We had a chance to catch up."

Marcus smiled at her and sauntered over to the wheel. The rest of the crew loaded one dinghy with dead aliens and readied another for safe passage to the island. The captain came over to the boats before the three boarded. He shook hands with John before he jumped into the dinghy. Then he hugged Eva warmly before lifting Susan into the boat with a mighty embrace.

"Keep checking with the sunstone necklace," he told her. "It will provide the light we need to see our way out of the darkness."

****

When they reached the Lexington cooperative, Susan scheduled a party for Christmas Day at Buckham Tavern. The timing marked almost two weeks after the aliens dumped the tea in Boston Harbor. The Sons of Liberty claimed responsibility for the Boston Tea Party in the Massachusetts Spy. The aliens could not read or write and so their claim remained undisputed. Susan augmented her promise to John Parker, and all beverages were on-the-house. Having worked so hard to live to attend the party, Susan added food to the beverage list.

John met Susan at the bar as she poured him a glass of sparkling wine. Looking warmly into her eyes, he told her, "I think that we should spend the night in that portal to the amber room tonight."

"Hmm," Susan murmured, glancing at the party goers filling the room. Looking down to wipe the counter clean, she responded, "I don't know. Eva is distressed. She misses the captain."

"Then I'll stay and stand guard," he announced.

"Great idea," Susan said, taking a couple of gulps of liquid from her glass. "Protect Eva."

"Eva," he shouted. "Can you watch the place while we post a few guard units?"

Eva appeared from behind a curtain and filled Susan's cup with more red wine. Susan left the filled glass as John took her hand in his. He guided her around the bar as if taking the lead in a dance. Together they headed for two men standing near the front door.

"Hello Mr. Caleb Harrington and dear brother Henry Parker. Please watch Miss Eva and the stash of liquor at the bar. Make sure that she doesn't get away without a marriage proposal from either of you tonight."

"Hopefully, she'll be able to make up her mind," Susan interjected.

"What?" Caleb turned around and questioned Henry. "You've been seeing Miss Eva, too?"

"She has been pulling double duty at musket drills," John told them both. "She wants children."

"A lot of children," Susan added.

John removed the bottle of wine clutched in his brother's hand. Freed from the bottle, Henry raced to the bar to beat out Caleb, who had already positioned himself as close as possible to Eva. John tugged on Susan's arm and directed her out the front door.

"We've done our duty," he remarked, eyeing the collection at the bar over his shoulder. When they were out of hearing distance, he said, "Let's go enjoy the night. We have a lot more work to do in that portal you showed me."

Chapter Twenty-Four

The heavens above are reflected

In the eyes of those

Who see it below

Reference Tune: *Wheel In The Sky*

----Journey

JOHN AWOKE THE next morning and found the country doctor standing over him. Fully dressed, Susan sat beside him on the bed. She held his hand as the physician spoke.

"It was quite a night, Mr. Parker. Your wife woke me early this morning," he began.

"Wife?" John asked.

Susan lightly patted his wrist. Glancing at her, he said, "Oh yes, I had her send for you."

Then he sunk back contentedly into the feathered pillows behind him.

"And a good thing you did," the doctor added. "You have tuberculosis. I'm glad we caught it. She knows the protocol."

The doctor quickly gathered his instruments as John shook his head behind his back. Susan waited patiently for the man to leave, then she removed her clothes. John drew back the blankets for her and she joined him underneath.

"You are going to have to take it easy," she said.

Curling his body around her, he said, "I had forgotten about your skills as a caregiver."

"Eva and I spent too much time working in the infirmary last year. I know better," she said.

"How much time did the doctor give me?" he asked.

"A year or two," she answered. "Make the most of it."

"I will," he answered holding her tightly.

Despite his condition, John continued to conduct military drills on the ground around Buckham Tavern. He and Susan continued to explore the portal to the amber room for protection. Meanwhile, Eva married Caleb before 1774 started. She moved out of the tavern, turning a house, three doors down, into a new home.

Nabby arrived in late January to show Susan the latest documentation on the alien attacks. She was accompanying her relation Joseph Adams to his new place in Lincoln, Massachusetts. Sitting at a table near the bar, the three reviewed the information.

"This particular breed of aliens is ancient. They are somehow connected to civilizations following the Fall of Eden. I think they called it Pangea," Joseph remarked.

"The civilization arose after the breakup of Pangea," Susan said. "I think the same aliens attacked this civilization."

"What was it called?" Nabby asked.

"I don't know. Let's call it post-Pangea," Susan said. "The alien issue should be addressed at the First Continental Congress this October."

"They are having it in Philadelphia," Joseph mentioned. "Despite its complicated social scene, the city appears to have some immunity from alien invasion."

"We need a system of government that deals with this ongoing situation," Nabby said.

"It is like all the other undeclared wars on American soil," Susan commented.

"If we don't define it, then it is easier to hide," Joseph said. "The patriots intend to use the aliens to their advantage. They are following the example of the imported Priory of Scion."

"That's in France," Susan commented.

"Yes, Sam told my father that the British ships were sent by General Gage who purposely harbored the aliens," Nabby said.

"Yes, it appears that Gage wants to replace Hutchison as master of the harbor," Joseph added. "It is a matter of parliamentary procedure."

"So parliament is working with the Priory of Scion," Susan observed. Rising from the table, she collected the papers and prepared to leave the tavern.

"Where are you going?" Nabby asked.

"I am going to visit the Parker farm. They are caring for John there. Besides his father, he has a brother and a sister in the minute forces," she added, rushing around the tavern. "They need this information, so we can prepare for the eventual land attack."

"How's John?" Joseph questioned.

"His father came for him after Christmas. I haven't seen him since. He'll probably get out more when the weather warms." Susan pulled on her coat and hat. Turning to Joseph, she said, "I want to travel with you halfway to Lincoln. Come back next week, and I'll show you the draft for the constitution. I've been working on it lately."

"Let's meet weekly before the October congress in Philadelphia," Joseph said. "I'll come under the cover of darkness."

Nabby and Joseph quickly donned their jackets and hurried outside to the wagon waiting near the barn. Susan sat in the covered area near the front bench where Joseph drove the horses. Next to Joseph on the bench, Nabby covered herself in several blankets to protect herself from the frosty afternoon. When they were halfway to Joseph's home in Lincoln, Susan jumped out of the wagon. She journeyed the rest of the way on foot. Half a mile away, she knocked on the door of the main cabin. Jonas, John's father, opened the door and ushered her inside. He immediately ushered her over to a dining table near the fire. John and several members of the Parker family were gathered around the table, performing small tasks befitting the season. Some knitted, some whittled, and some read.

Keeping his poker face, John pulled out a chair for Susan as they quickly commenced with a business discussion. She lightly touched his hand in reply and then abruptly withdrew before anyone else in the room noticed the subtlety. Then Susan related the details of her meeting with Nabby and Joseph. Jonas stroked his chin as he listened, then he observed, "If the Priory of Scion has entered the picture, then we are still at war with France. We must be prepared for aliens, demons, Frenchmen, British soldiers, and pirates."

"Yes, they are leaving their secret warehouse at Boston Harbor and staying at the Publick House at Sturbridge. They intend to build a village there," John said, eyeing Susan. He added, "We are in-between."

Susan nodded. "This is the piece I've been missing. General Gage and parliament are allies with the French priory."

"Although they dislike each other, the Sons of Liberty and loyalists in Boston commons are banking with the financiers of parliament. The priory might attack Bunker Hill, but they won't touch Boston Commons. They already occupy it. Henry Knox is marrying the daughter of a loyalist, one that has parliament's approval."

Susan added, "They didn't invite anyone from the Green Dragon Tavern to the wedding. The overtures are political."

The discussion was interrupted by a heavy knock on the door. Jonas rose to answer it, and invited the guest inside the house. The cloaked man pulled the hood from his face, revealing himself.

Sitting down at the table, John Andre unraveled himself from his scarves and woolens. He began as Jonas brought him a cup of hot mead. "I have great news. The French king intends to support your mission against the priory."

"You have perfect timing. How did you know we were here?" Susan asked.

"Nathan told me about the priory's secret warehouse on the harbor. Eva told me about the party on Christmas Day. I figured that you would come here after Joseph visited the tavern," he answered.

Susan glanced at John Parker and took a deep breath. Turning away from his blank stare, she explained, "This is what happens after you grow up on a ship together. Your actions become predictable." Then she confronted John Andre, "Will the secret du roi join the Blue Heron forces?"

"Even if they succeed in killing the king with smallpox and keep our top spy d'Eon exiled in England, we can continue our support. The Comte Charles de Broglie is handling it. He is trying to bring in his top royal officer Lafayette. Lafayette can out-maneuver George Washington when the pirates hand him command of the continental army. The captain is already working with the French financier Beaumarchais for ammunitions and supplies."

"Great," Jonas commented. "We can hide the munitions in Concord, after we bring them up the river to the Lexington Bridge. I am in charge of the minute forces in Concord, and have several plans developed already."

Chapter Twenty-Five

The final analysis is always left up to the individual

Reference Tune: *Who Will Save Your Soul*

----Jewel

KING LOUIS XV died from smallpox in May 1774. In the same month General Gage replaced Hutchison and put Boston under military rule. It was two months after the courts deprived Beaumarchais of his civil rights through a setup. By the Fourth of July, Marbie's Inn in New York passed the Orangetown Resolutions, which boasted an intolerance for both the King of England and his parliament. While the most vocal and violent colonists continued to bemoan the economy, Eva and Caleb prepared for the birth of their first child, who was due in early October. At Buckham Tavern, Susan, Joseph, and Nabby continued prepping for the First Continental Congress, which had been moved to September after Sam Adams pushed for a boycott of British goods. Though many of the colonists knew about the May boycott, few seemed ready for action. The Boston town meeting brought the committee of correspondence into the public eye, which leveraged the rancorous Sons of Liberty into civility.

"I thought that Loyalists operated Marbie Inn in New York, but now it appears that the Priory of Scion and their alien sponsors run it," Joseph commented when he met with Susan during the summer. "They are setting the tone for the First Continental Congress meeting."

"The captain told John Andre that no ship goes near Tappan after the alien attack on Ellis Island," Susan mentioned. "The Dutch East India Company wants to control commerce on the Hudson River. It is their way of scaring away competitors. Now they plan to use the colonists to attack England."

"It will be a contest between Patrick Henry's Virginia Association plus Sam's boycott versus the Orangetown Resolutions," Joseph commented. "I suggest that we get to Philadelphia early and pay a visit to Deborah Reed in late August."

"Is that wise?" Susan asked. "I understand that Dr. Joseph Warren is holding another meeting at Faneuil Hall. His various committees of correspondence resolve to declare themselves independent of British authority."

"Such action is like creating another undeclared war," Joseph observed. "Warren's legions from Suffolk want us to buy goods from the United India Company instead. Henry Knox has already been drilling his own company militia in Boston Commons. General Gage ignores him because he is directing the conflict away from the wealthy homes in Boston. Knox is fortifying Breed Hill or Bunker Hill on the Charlestown peninsula. It's a setup."

"You are right, Joseph," Susan stated. "It is best that we stay away from such physicians as Dr. Rush and Dr. Warren. The captain told me that they have been experimenting with biologic implants in conjunction with the galvanizing techniques being developed in England. Someday someone will write a book about how some crazy Transylvanian scientist uses electricity to restore function to dead body parts."

"They'll name the revived corpse after Dr. Franklin, except it will have a Transylvanian translation like Franklinstein."

"Okay, back to order, naturally," Susan said. "We ignore Warren and his mayhem for the moment, and pass along the documents to Patrick Henry, who will be in Philadelphia."

"No, under the circumstances, we should stay with the Native Americans," Joseph said. "We probably would not be safe at Franklin Court."

"In that case, we should just stay on the Camden," Susan remarked. "The captain moved his trading business to Philadelphia after the alien attack. We could bring munitions to Concord on our return trip. I'll travel independently with the supply line."

****

When they arrived at Philadelphia, Susan met Deborah Reed at City Tavern. Using the secret room with the portal to the amber room for protection, the two women discussed the latest ongoings.

"The colonists want to start making their own money," Deborah began. "The delegation from Orangetown wants a national currency."

"We aren't a nation, yet," Susan remarked. "The United India Company wants a corporate model with an economic exchange rate that benefits them."

"No, real exchange involved. It will wreck our present system of trade."

"What do you suggest?" Susan asked.

"I want to introduce you to John Marshall. He is interested in starting the minute forces in Culpeper, Virginia," Deborah said. "They want to reorganize themselves under the Committees of Safety instead of the Committees of Correspondence."

"That's a shrewd move to defeat the Orangetown complaints and Galloway proposals that want to mire the new government," Susan observed.

"Though Virginia gentry consider him a slaveholder. It is only a cover-up for his role in the Freedom Trail to City Tavern. Nobody notices the high turnover on his modest place beside the monumental homes of Madison, Jefferson, Washington, Randolph, and the others. He is a young law student with a refined moral conscience and possesses an idealistic curiosity that surpasses even Yates's. God bless."

"When do they arrive?" Susan asked.

"I told them to come after an hour."

"Great, they can help me unload the books that I borrowed. Some can go home with you. Some will be delivered by my driver to Patrick Henry to return to the various libraries in town. The other books I will send with a note to Thomas Jefferson, who is staying near Carpenter Hall. I'll let him know that the Duke of York took Tom Jefferson with him on a tour of France. It will be a great educational experience for Thomas's son. He is such a bright young man."

No sooner than the itinerary was mentioned than a strapping young man almost six years old appeared in the doorway. Nabby and Joseph swarmed into the room from behind him and hugged Susan and Mrs. Reed. An older man followed them through the door. Placing his cane aside in his other hand, he warmly shook the women's hands.

"I brought one of my cousins from Virginia with me," the young man said after introducing himself as John Marshall. "This is the man who runs cover in the assembly for Patrick Henry. He is like the yin to Patrick's yang.

Please meet the president of the First Continental Congress, Mr. Peyton Randolph. His election is just a political formality. We are leaving nothing to chance at this crucial meeting, so that the pirates don't run away with it."

The group of seven sat down at the table, where Susan briefed them on the latest happenings and developments. After the meeting, John Marshall helped Susan unload Franklin's books into Mrs. Reed's carriage. The rest of the books were divided between two additional carriages and directed to the places where Henry and Jefferson stayed. Then John Marshall hopped in the emptied wagon and took the reins. Susan sat beside them on the driver's bench as they drove through town to the Philadelphia Harbor where they could find the Camden. Their lighthearted travel was interrupted by the thunderous sound of galloping horses' hooves coming their way from around the wagon. Without saying a word, Marshall slid out of the driver's seat and met the hooded riders with his hands in the air. Susan jumped out of the wagon at the opposite end. Falling slightly when she hit the ground, the shawl over her head fell over her face, concealing her appearance temporarily from the attackers. Limping, she walked away from the wagon as the hooded men listened to the masked rider leading the attack. The voice behind the mask was a woman's, and she told the men to search the wagon for books, slaves, and papers.

A ray from the setting sun bounced off the sunstone crystal and blinded the horses gathered around the wagon. The men preparing to torch the wagon caught fire as their horse reared. The five horses pulling the wagon bolted for the water's edge looming in the distance. Susan ran fast from the scene and hid in an alley a half mile away.

"Here," Marshall said softly as he waved at her across a cobblestone street. "How's the ankle?"

"I'll feel it tomorrow, though the motion seems to have quickly adjusted it." Then she added, "Follow me, I know a cabin on the outskirts of town. It is the safest place right now. The horses will go straight to the Camden. The captain will be able to spot us through his scope on the bluff. He knows its location."

They reached the cabin before darkness, and signaled the Camden from the bluff. The next morning, the captain and Mrs. Reed knocked on the door of the cabin. Susan quickly opened the door as Marshall did his best to make the place hospitable in the southern tradition. He brewed some tea from herbs that they had collected that morning and offered a plate of berries and fruit.

Accompanying them were Peyton Randolph, Patrick Henry, and a dark-skinned woman. Peyton pushed the woman forward and introduced her. "Meet my friend and ally, Miss Lydia Broadnax. She is a scholar from the George Wythe House in Virginia. George and his wife stayed at home to put together the state militia."

Those assembled in the tiny group went directly to business. Mrs. Reed began, "The woman who led the attack on you was Franklin's first wife. She is from the Sassoon family, who has pledged allegiance to financiers of the Red Hand."

"House of Roth?" Susan questioned.

"Further back," Lydia responded. "In Prussia, they are buried with the sign of the goose."

"Gans?" Marshall asked.

"Joachim Gans, the descendant of a British profiteer who brokered the arrangement between Queen Elizabeth and her pirate, Captain Drake. Nothing changes in the Gans family."

Chapter Twenty-Six

Sometimes it all comes down
To one final resolution

Reference Tune: *Too Late For Goodbyes*
----Julian Lennon

"YES, GANS AND the pirate Drake worked with the United India Company. With the help of aliens, they attacked the colony at Roanoke, Virginia. They stole valuable technology in metallurgy from the Native Americans," Lydia explained.

"Paul Revere is using a similar technique in his ship repairs. He is the only one who is using copper sheets in this manner," the captain said. "The problem with the technology is that it is from the same guild. It incriminates Revere."

"What do you mean?" Susan asked.

"Franklin met the sister of Miriam Simon at a fraternity party. William was the result of the counter-Regulan Star Lodge creating liaisons with the Antient Lodge. Germaine, or the immortal Sauron, is the inspiration for the constitution of the lodge. It is this constitution that Hayman Solomon, another Gans agent, intends to fund."

"I understand why they don't like our efforts," Susan said. "There's competition."

"The father of former Governor Keith, the man who had Benjamin detained in England, worked with Andre's unit in Germany. Their headquarters in England is the Devils Tavern in London. Benjamin joined the Hellfire Club with John Wilkes while he worked in England. When he returned to America, he published the Antient constitution along with his proposal for a paper currency."

"They intend to infuse the currency of America with Germaine's occult symbols," Marshall observed. Taking a deep breath, he added, "So Franklin's first wife is extorting him."

"He learned how to play the game," Deborah added. "She knows what you are doing and led the attack. Most of the attendees at the congress will be buried at the churches of the lodges here in Philadelphia. Their souls linked."

"Well, here," Susan said, unfolding a document that she pulled from a pocket in her skirt. "Instead of a Bill of Rights, we have The Fundamentals of a Civilization. Please review it for the presentation at the congress." Then she produced another folded piece of paper from the folds of her shawl. She put it next to the paper entitled Fundamentals of a Civilization. "I am sure that you are all familiar with the Declaration of Independence. Here is our Declaration of Interdependence, which we will divide in halves and hide until it becomes safe to pursue."

People gathered around the documents and passed the papers amongst themselves.

Mr. Peyton Randolph commented, "Our opponents will try to produce a document that resembles the Magna Carta of Liberties."

"Are you referring to the charter that Robin Hood used to subjugate King John?" Susan asked.

"It resulted from the earls' revolt against the king," Peyton commented. "London eventually used the charter to declare self-rule."

Susan continued, "The natives that the Romans displaced used their own Roman laws against them with some success. I want to go beyond tit for tat. The constitution will be completed with the help of John Marshall. We shall have it done by the end of the congress. I think that we can stay and work on it here at the cabin."

Fundamentals of a Civilization

Preamble for the United America
The people of the continent are represented by their initiative in Philadelphia, Pennsylvania, preceding the first congress on this continent, on the sixth of September, one thousand seven hundred and seventy-four.

Resolved by the Committees of Correspondence and the Continental militias.

Component I
Only those religions, organizations, and institutions in harmony with the spirit of the planet are tolerated.

Component II
Creatures great and small shall have the power to communicate without imposed restriction. The communication must address the recipient's ability to hear.

Component III

All beings assuming the human form must be given safe passage and travel.

Component IV

All beings have the option to pursue nonviolent courses, except in cases of inaction.

Component V

Human beings must be able to join for purposes of appropriate contact.

Component VII

All creatures great and small have the right to reproductive freedom, including the choice of consenting partners. These freedoms must be life-supporting, sustainable, and in harmony with the balances inherent on the planet.

Component VII

The use of power depends on the circumstances defined and checked by those abiding by the Fundamentals of a Civilization described.

****

DECLARATION OF INTERDEPENDENCE

By initiative in Philadelphia, Pennsylvania, preceding the first congress on this continent, on the sixth of September, one thousand seven hundred and seventy-four.

The course of human events concerning this American continent demands a call to action. We, the people declare our spirits free to pursue destinies befitting the divine intent. All creatures are created equal with varying degrees of spirit. America is the continent destined for those with spirit, not a patriotism blinded by competing interests.

We declare ourselves free from the commercial interests that wound our spirit. We wish to promote the human family without royal obligations. The abundant, natural spirit of this continent must be preserved.

We declare our present situation intolerable. The present oligarchies ruin our health and wound our spirit. The businesses conducted on this terrain have become unsafe and unfair. For these reasons, we will fight to preserve our integrity and save our souls.

We declare resistance to any attempt to restrict or impose another will on our lives. The sacrifices have been many, and the limit has been reached. While no violence will be pursued for its violence, we will protect the boundaries of the humans deciding not to submit.

We declare our lives inoperable under the present circumstances of intolerance. The unfair treatment and enslavement of a human spirit is repulsive. This will not be bred on this terrain with its resulting damage to all of humanity.

We declare our heartfelt interest in forming new bonds with the nations that encouraged refugees to settle on this continent. Our new nation will incorporate those indigenous tribes uncontaminated by an alien spirit. Those without a soul will be given safe passage from the continent, if not the planet. We choose to handle such matters in harmony with the nation's vitality, which includes the terrain.

We declare our own ability to govern ourselves as we succeed as a nation. All present properties belong to us. They shall be traded, seized, or compensated at fair market prices according to the manner in which we are collectively treated and recognized as a national continent. Any entity threatening this action will be exiled.

These truths are undeniable and valid. They will forever haunt the inhabitants of this continent if not addressed appropriately.

Those present in the room signed the documents and celebrated the deal.

Chapter Twenty-Seven

Love is one of

The few things in life that persists

Reference Tune: *A Thousand Years*

----Christina Perri

PEYTON RANDOLPH POCKETED both documents and the group left Susan and Marshall to work on the constitution. Mrs. Reed left some food supplies to add to whatever they collected on their own. When they finished their work, Susan left for the Camden under the cover of darkness.

"There is a man on board from Vermont," the captain told Susan when she stepped on the boat. "He's been fighting the aliens in New York and the governor wants his head."

"Welcome to the club. I can name at least two governors that pursued me. One lost his leg at City Tavern," Susan said, scanning the deck for the sight of the newcomer. Turning to the captain, she questioned, "Why is he here?"

A tall, freckled man in his mid-thirties with reddish hair stepped from the shadows near the ship's wheel. "I resigned from the Masonic Lodge that attacked you and Mr. John Marshall after you left City Tavern. Your fighting maneuvers impressed me. I want to be your friend."

The captain quipped, "Beware. She is a spiritual warrior of the highest persuasion. You won't know what you've lost until she's gone."

Susan rolled her eyes at the captain while the man politely bowed with a smile. He introduced himself, "My name is Remember Baker. When I don't command a company of Green Mountain Boys, I handle my cousin Ethan Allen's legalities against the government of New York."

"Why bother me?" she questioned, placing her hand over the hilt of a small sword strapped to her waist.

"I have some additions to your constitution," he said as he shook his head and glanced at the wooden floor. "I mean our constitution."

"Oh, now it is our constitution," Susan observed without a hint of intonation. She glanced at the stars above and looked at the captain.

"Why did you let him on your ship?" she asked the captain.

"Every misguided male deserves a chance," he told her. "He came in peace and now he wants to promote our work. I think that he has some insight on the dark occultism that threatens our present existence."

"We'll serve to protect it, too," he rejoined. "I promise that you will remember me in a more positive light."

Susan turned on her heels and motioned him toward her. He followed Susan to the ship's kitchen. She produced the document from her skirt pocket and placed it on the table. Remember studied the document following every line with the extended fingers on his right hand. Part of his thumb was missing.

When he finished, he stepped away and explained, "It's my lucky Green thumb. It senses the life imbued in physical objects. I think you have a great legal framework here. My suggestions will procure even greater immunity from the lost tribes of Israel. Most of the tribes are degrading the human family. They chose to become occult pirates."

"It sounds like you have the angle on it," Susan commented.

The next day, Susan handed the document over to Patrick Henry. "A descendent of the Spencers came over to help with the rest. He lives with his merry men on Green Mountain. It is in Vermont."

"They had to come out of the convent sometime, especially with the Henry VIII edict resulting in the dissolution of the monasteries," Patrick piped. "Robin's grandfather, the Earl of Huntingdon, doubled as Waltheof, a Catholic saint and martyr of cult proportions. The Welsh baron's opposition to King John, the ruler of Wales, began with the English revolt of the earls against William the Conqueror."

"The hood of Robin was nothing more than a monastic cover," Susan observed. "The Priory of Scion seeded itself into other continents. The priory brought in aliens."

"English law dealt with the alien issue by turning all churches in Britain into the Church of England."

"I can see why the Spencers left. They disguised themselves as Pilgrims."

"The aliens have an ongoing war with the Pilgrims. This is why they seized New York. Now New York attacks Green Mountain."

He promised to take the document immediately to Peyton Randolph's bedside. The president of the congress had fallen ill, perhaps due to poisoning. Only Patrick and a few others knew about the situation. The constitution read:

THE CONSTITUTION OF UNITED AMERICA

We the people of the American continent to deliver ourselves from the surrounding dark chaos chose a government aimed at self-determinism and self-reliance.

Article I.

The government should resemble a living structure with four main branches: citizens, legislative, judicial, and executive. The life of the structure shall reflect the existence of the people in a sustainable manner. The main body represents the collective, while the foundation is described in the Fundamentals of a Civilization.

Article II.

Section 1.

Citizens must be a member of the human family. They are defined as those who inhabit the terrain after having passed through the birth canal. New beings, such as those salvaged through various forms of human vivisection, must inhabit the terrain for at least two years before seeking citizenship. A citizen must be fifteen years old to participate in the voting process, and be able to provide valid identification and proof of terrain habitation. Special consideration will be given those of propagating age who assume responsibility for the documents defining the governance. No registration necessary for the voting process, except in cases of special elections when it becomes necessary for reasons of accountability.

Section 2.

Tribes of human families inhabiting the terrain may be treated as separate states. Tribes may gather as a collective to form a state. A person charged with treason, felony, or a crime shall, on demand of the judicial authority of the state, be held accountable. New states must prove themselves worthy to the collective represented in the legislative branch. A simple majority is sufficient to bring in a new state. The executive and judiciary branches protect the states gathered in the union.

Article III.

The legislative branch consists of a congress divided into a House of Representatives and a Senate. Legislators must make the laws consistent with the Fundamentals of a Civilization.

Section 1.

The House of Representatives shall be composed of members chosen every six years by citizens of voting age. Each state is entitled to elect one representative. There should be one representative for every four thousand people in a state, or a proportional relationship such that the number of total representatives does not exceed the workable number of five hundred. Efficiency and productivity represent the people. The goal is not to govern, but to make government work. Representatives must be twenty-two-years old and be an inhabitant of their state for ten years. The House of Representatives shall choose their own speaker and officers.

Section 2.

There shall be two senators from each state appointed by the country's president for four year terms. A senator must have inhabited a state for five years and be twenty years old to serve. The president of the Senate must be elected by the House of Representatives, and only votes in cases of a tie. The Senate shall choose all other officers.

Section 3.

The legislative branch must meet at least once a year.

Article IV.

The executive branch is defined by the national election of a president with his chosen vice-president. The term is limited to four years, but there is no limit on reruns after the hiatus. The president must have inhabited the American continent for his or her lifetime, and be a citizen over twenty-eight-years old. The president executes the laws determined by the legislative division and defined by the judiciary branch.

Section 1.

The president serves as commander of the armed forces, demands opinions and clarifications from the executive departments, appoints ambassadors and officers, and may have appointees submit bills of governmental necessity to the legislators or cases pertaining to governmental necessity to the Supreme Court. Unnecessary bills or cases are grounds for impeachment as determined by the Supreme Court.

Section 2.

The senate may impeach the president by a simple majority. The Supreme Court may initiate impeachment through the House of Representatives, where a simple majority would be required.

Section 3.

The president, vice-president, and other civil officers shall be removed from office in cases of proven death and disability or conviction of treason, bribery, high crimes, and misdemeanors. They may resign at any time and be replaced by voters. The vice president replaces the president for the duration of the term. If both officers must be replaced, then a special election is held while the President of the Senate assumes the executive office temporarily.

Article VI.

Section 1.

The judicial branch of the government consists of a Supreme Court, state, and tribal or municipal courts where the judges are elected by each jurisdiction for four-year terms. They must be fifty years of age and have inhabited the American continent for the lifetime. Ten members from a lottery are chosen for each case. The decision is made by simple majority. One additional judge is required to monitor the process, arbitrate proceedings, and settle ties.

Section 2.

The president may propose amendments to the constitution or the Supreme Court may have an appointee suggest an amendment as a result of a decision. Amendments must have the approval of the House of Representatives by two-thirds of the vote and the Senate by simple majority.

Article VII

States must agree to the constitution in order to be considered a state in the Union. A simple majority is acceptable by those elected and appropriated to previously-formed state militias or state committees of correspondence.

Article VIII

The executive, legislative, and judicial branches of service are paid positions. The funds must be collected before the office is assumed and the compensation must remain invariant until the term completed.

Later in the day, Patrick Henry returned to the Camden with a note from Peyton Randolph.

By golly, I think we've got it. We're off to a great start, and can figure out how to finance the thing after we talk to Beaumachias. Right now, we are simply a land of people running on donations and natural abundance.

-Peyte

Two weeks later, Peyton died from internal bleeding near the close of the congressional session. Leaving town before the funeral service, Ethan escorted Susan back to Concord with a wagonload of military supplies. Mrs. Reed attended the funeral and died from a stroke that December. To avoid capture by the occult Mason group that he left, Ethan remained at the Lexington cooperative for the winter.

Chapter Twenty-Eight

Sometimes it's all relative

There's bad,

Which can be considered God's play

And then there is EVIL,

Which is really bad

Reference Tune*: Bad To The Bone*

----George Thorogood and The Destroyers

BY THE START of 1775, Eva and Caleb expected their second child. Remember stayed at Buckham Tavern and oversaw military drills while John Parker convalesced. Susan taught him a few maneuvers involving the use of awareness and illusion, which some people termed magic.

"I don't know if we have the strength to regain New York. The loss of Mrs. Reed and Mr. Randolph is discouraging," Remember commented doing a wintery morning as they drilled. A tear fell from the corner of his eye and he quickly wiped it away before it froze. Facing Susan, he told her, "I haven't seen techniques like these since I was a small boy. My father used a similar style."

"What happened in New York?" Susan questioned Remember as they walked together by the river meandering its way underneath the Lexington Bridge. The bridge bordered the property of the cooperative and marked the unofficial entrance. There was several feet of snow on the ground and part of the river remained frozen. Susan dropped Remember's hand to investigate the current surfacing at the edge of the ice.

Rather than continue waiting for his answer, she filled the air with more words. "I feel sad and stuck in a freezing current like a block of ice. With the passing of the elders, the momentum seems gone. There is no one older and wiser in these legal matters to tell us whether we are on track."

Tapping on the white cube in front of her, she broke a piece away and watched the freed water move swiftly down river. There in the deep blue crystal water glistening in the wintery sun, she saw her own reflection staring back at her. A shiver ran up her spine, and she shook her head to escape the image.

"It is getting warm," she told Remember, who stared down at her. His reflection also appeared in the darker cobalt hues of the melting ice. He stood motionless on the bank several feet above her. Susan remarked, "The water seems so refreshing. I've never seen it so sparkling."

"Fire to the mountain," he murmured. "I'll take the reflection back to the crags of Vermont."

"What do you mean?" she asked, rising from the river's edge to face him.

"There's a spark of life in Lexington that can't be extinguished," he told her as he gathered her in his arms to kiss her. "I want to take it home to Vermont."

She squirmed under his embrace and stepped softly away from him. "About New York?"

"It's more than a minor land dispute," he answered. "The Pilgrims were the first settlers to retrieve the land from beings that didn't belong on the planet. The aliens infected agents of the East India Company, which belonged to the sons of Abraham. The Brahmins degraded into pirates. So it is the same with those representing the company in New York."

"This isn't just a thinly disguised war with aliens," Susan observed. "It is a confrontation with the scattered human refugees from the attack on the Tower of Babylon."

"Dan's tribe and a daughter from the House of David survived with intact souls," he said. He thrust his hands in his pockets to brace against the cold, bitter wind kicking up snowflakes in the air. Scanning the fields in the distance, he told her, "It is about spiritual survival of the soul during these cold times. The time of the tribal pirates is limited. They have already cast their lot with the aliens. We'll find them later collected in the graveyards around Christ Church and the neighboring synagogue in Philadelphia."

"That's cold," Susan remarked as she motioned him back to the tavern.

"The rest of us will go like a river, and return to the planet in a different form," he said as he walked beside her on the white field.

They punched their boots through the snow and made a trail to the front door. Heat from the fire quickly warmed their faces as they peered inside the front door. Inside, John Andre sat in a chair by the hearth. He looked up from his book and greeted the couple.

"I have news from Boston," he told them. "Dr. Warren and John Hancock have established a provincial government." Closing his book shut, he added, "Mrs. Gage, our informant, says that her husband intends to declare Massachusetts in a state of rebellion."

"Her husband is the British general who replaced Governor Hutchison. Reconciliation with Britain is a foolish notion," Remember commented, warming himself by the fire.

Susan sat down and removed her wet boots. She observed, "Two roads are emerging. The distinction between the paths has become a legal definition."

Andre lifted his head and strained his neck to listen. Remember patted her shoulder gently. Sensing their unspoken encouragement, Susan continued. "The colonists are blind. They perceive England as a benevolent parent, one that can understand reason. Parliament and General Gage view us as a military rebellion. By their laws and assessments, we are treasonous."

"The punishment is death." Andre observed, "That's their justification for Yates's murder"

"The three legislators accused me of treason at City Tavern," Susan added. "However, they were saving me for a ritual that only illicit occult organizations employ."

"We are not dealing with just another army," Remember commented. "I assure you that dark occultists are behind the attacks. What does the magic in your sunstone crystal have to offer?"

Standing in front of the fire, Susan consulted the sunstone crystal. A flame from the fire leaped into the air, and became reflected in the dimensions of the stone. A Blue fairy appeared in the room behind them.

"Remember me," she began in a familiar, soft voice. "The MidEarth promised to protect the souls that died protecting it. The three of you form a new guild. Do not fight the rushing current of events trapped underneath the ice. Go with the flow. Let the current take you away."

Then the Blue fairy nodded at the blue hue that suddenly had appeared in the flame. She faded as the intensity in the hearth increased. The three turned their attention to the fire and watched it die down.

"Once the ice is broken, there will be no turning back," Remember observed. Immediately he rose to his feet and rushed to gather his belongings from the tavern. "From Boston they will come here first. The two roads represent separate financial paths."

"That is what occurred to me," Susan remarked quietly as she assumed her chores behind the counter. "If they have pursued Beauchmais, then they must know about our munitions in Concord. Though new funding venues surfaced in Philadelphia, our friends suddenly died under suspicious circumstances. Deborah and Peyton enjoyed good health at the beginning of the convention."

Remember said, "The Brahmins want a war that will render the continent in their debt. It's another form of exploitation. It was perfected over the ages by the pirates now operating the Spice Route."

Looking at the red, yellow, orange, embers in the fire, John Andre added, "The royals of France want to fund the fighting that America will do on our behalf. After the assassination attempt on Louis XV, we realized that these Brahmins wanted to oppress us all. We must work together with the royal descendants, who have already fled to this nation."

"My ancestor was the Bishop Patrick," Remember said. "Another ancestor, Robin Hood, rebelled against the persecution of his monasteries."

"Now that they have us corralled on this continent, there is no other escape left," Susan said. "We must get the war officially declared. If they want a revolution, we'll give them one."

Remember approached Susan and gently readjusted the necklace around her with a touch of affection. Holding the sunstone crystal in his hand, he asked, "Tell me about the powers of your necklace. I heard that it saved you several times from an Arachnid 33 crucifixion."

Andre sighed, rubbing his legs for circulation as he stared into the fire again. "Someone stole the other half of the necklace. When it was fully intact, the necklace only offered guidance to safety. In India, we ran from the British army. General Gage is an evil man, unlike any the continent has seen."

"Fort Ticonderoga will be one of the first targets," Remember announced before leaving the hearth to collect his things. "When the revolution becomes official, General Gage will attempt to seize control of the Hudson River. Their commercial interests have become as crystal clear as a stream in winter."

Susan paused for a moment and watched him pack. Then she returned to her work behind the counter. John Andre resumed reading his book.

Remember stopped to kiss her cheek before exiting. She turned around and threw her arms around his neck. Staring into his eyes, she said, "You must hurry to claim Fort Ticonderoga. I will have Andre inform the captain of your plans. He has his sights on the Hudson, too."

Chapter Twenty-Nine

What about those life-supporting decisions?

Is it really life that is chosen?

Life moves

Life flows

Life works

Life heals

What is life?

What marks its end?

Reference Tune: *Tainted Love*

----Soft Cell

AFTER HE LEFT, Susan addressed John Andre, "I want you give a note to Mrs. Gage. Tell her that if her husband's troops cross the Lexington Bridge, I will shoot to protect our convalescents. It is not a declaration of war."

John Andre opened his eyes wide, but he remained silent. "If you open fire, the British will declare war."

Susan rose from her chair by the fire to retrieve a pen and paper. Briefly looking down at the floor before scribbling a note, she told John Andre, "I want to define my destiny and draw boundaries. The British will never murder another one of my patients without a fight. We need a legitimate war for our own protection."

She handed the note to John Andre as he left the hearth to put on his jacket and scarf. He kissed her on the cheek after placing the note in his chest pocket. Susan lingered in his presence and whispered in his ear, "There is another reason."

She pulled away from him, and explained, "If Dr. Warren is truly in league with General Gage, then he will find a reason to lure British troops here. This well-placed note will lure out the traitors as well. If Lexington falls into the hands of the British, nothing will make sense any more. Be careful that you don't get caught in the cow dung."

John Andre nodded and left. The blank expression on his face told Susan that he had not quite followed her reasoning. She let him go without any further explanation.

Two weeks later, Parliament declared Massachusetts in a state of rebellion. In response, Patrick Henry stirred the halls of Virginia with the words, "Give me liberty or give me death." Parliament followed with an order for General Gage to forcibly suppress open rebellions. The carte blanche command reached Gage by early April. John Andre returned to Lexington the same week with a written reply from Mrs. Gage. Having gained enough strength to protect Andre on his travels, John Parker accompanied him. The men met Susan foraging herbs at the base of the bridge. She looked up at the riders when they arrived. The horses stilled as John Andre handed her the reply from Boston.

Susan opened the sealed envelope and read the letter; Andre filled her in on the latest details. "Dr. Warren, the president of the provincial government in Boston, decided to hold the next meeting at the Codhouse in Lincoln, Massachusetts. Both John Hancock and Sam Adams plan to attend.

The British have already issued a warrant for their arrest on the grounds of treason."

Susan nodded silently. She simultaneously listened and read the letter. After he finished speaking, she waved the note in the air. Avoiding his stare, she told them, "Mrs. Gage must be in some difficulty now. Her husband wrote this letter. His response is a confirmation that he will shoot those protecting Lexington."

She handed the note to John Andre. He reviewed the response. John Parker jumped off his horse. Without reading General Gage's intention, he told them, "I want to be a Blue Heron and take charge of my own destiny. My relationship with England is done. No reconciliation is possible."

"We learned that the British have already started their march to Lexington," Andre said softly before presenting the letter to Parker. "Parliament has already sent its financiers to create a war and establish new businesses in the aftermath. That is what we saw taking shape in Philadelphia."

Susan looked at Parker directly. She glanced at the other man before telling him, "Andre and I can recall the words of another messenger. She advised us to take up the sword and fight."

Parker handed the letter back to Susan, who placed it in a pocket before resuming her work. "I'll have the others hold back their fire when the British cross Lexington Bridge."

"I will fire to protect the property from trespassing British troops," Susan told him. "War has not been declared officially. They have no business here. I am not fighting to provoke the British and hand Parliament their war. The colonists will not support rebels."

Andre observed, "The massacres and skirmishes between the British and patriots have not brought the colonists into the war. The Sons of Liberty failed in that regard. France and other nations will not sympathize with the rule of an angry mob."

"Blatant aggression without any attempt to settle disputes will explode into a revolution," Parker said. "We must make ourselves clear."

"Actions speak louder than words," Susan stated. "I think I can produce that shot, though I may not live to see the resulting revolution."

"I can produce a well-disciplined militia to counter the redcoats," Parker said. "It will look like a war before a shot is heard."

"Enough said," Andre commented, shaking his head. "The resulting revolution will distract the opposition in France. Versailles is the seat of political power in the world. This should release Beaumachais and other international financiers, who will invest in America to ensure their own freedom. If the colonists lose, then the spirit of the planet will not recover."

"We already know what these evil forces did in India and Europe," Susan mentioned. "It no longer is just a matter of losing one's home, family, or life."

Then she left them to consult Nathan. Meeting him at the two-room house, she embraced him and told him about the Gage letters. Greg played with some wooden toys below their feet. He held her as tears streaked down her face.

Susan told him, "My recent tryst with John Parker unveiled the depths of his understanding and loyalty. He remains confused, and refuses to face many desperate truths. He hides our romantic relationship from his father, which means that we've been betrayed by both John Hancock and Sam Adams." Taking a deep breath, she whispered in Nathan's ear, "I only regret that I have only one life to give the Blue Herons. Sometimes I would like to fly away. I cannot think of anything else but to hold my ground. You must must escape and join forces with the women from the Varnum family. They have been working with the Wowenocks for generations. Hurry, and get them to the capitol at Annapolis, before the assassins in Philadelphia hand the revolution over to John Hancock's financiers for their revisions."

"I will find you in another life," he said. "I'll waddle to you out of your dreams, and you will recognize the love we shared." Then he kissed her softly and dried her tears. "Remember me."

By the next week, British troops learned of the provincial meeting in Lincoln, Massachusetts. They openly announced their intention to capture Sam Adams and John Hancock as they organized for battle. News of their march towards Lexington Bridge and the munitions supplies in Concord reached those raising the flag of the Blue Heron. When they crossed the bridge in front of Buckham Tavern and Susan opened fire as promised. British troops responded with well-aimed fire. Of the eighty people gathered for the Lexington militia, fifteen were immediately slaughtered. The others fled the grounds and buildings to reorganize on public property. This strategy minimized damaged to the cooperative. The Lexington battle ended in approximately an hour. After storming the tavern, the British dumped the bodies in the river underneath the bridge.

Women accounted for twenty percent of the minute forces led by Captain John Parker. Not only did the surviving relations wish to hide the gender identity of some of the fallen soldiers, but they wanted to bury the dead. Dressing as British soldiers, Eva and the captain ventured behind enemy lines. They found the bodies floating downstream and removed the necklace from Susan's neck. The necklace was given to the captain.

Unfortunately the magical properties of the ornament disappeared with her death. He was eventually killed while protecting the Hudson River.

Eva survived and delivered seven children. Near the end of the Revolutionary War, she succumbed to a yellow fever epidemic and perished. Her friend, John Andre, captured Paul Revere, who was leading the British to Codhouse. Unfortunately, a betrayal in the upper ranks resulted in Revere's release. John Hancock and Sam Adams barely escaped with their lives. Daniel Boone and Jonas Parker descended on the British soldiers on the way to Concord and repelled them. The munitions storage in Concord remained secured as the British returned to Boston to attack Bunker Hill. Having received early warning of the siege, Isaiah Thomson printed news about the Lexington-Concord Battle from his new location near Worcester, a town closer to the Sturbridge Publick House, the projected headquarters for the Priory of Scion. After the confrontation, the Revolution was officially declared. Joseph Adams fled to England for safety. The owners of the Codhouse shipped out to the West Indies. With the help of Paul Revere, Dr. Warren faked his death at Bunker Hill, and left for the West Indies. Later vacating his Concord cabin, Daniel Boone returned to his project in Kentucky, naming one of the towns that he founded Lexington. John Andre continued to secure negotiations with France, but George Washington and Benedict Arnold betrayed him. Rivingston's Gazette printed Andre's poem Cow Chase on the day they hung him. Prince Frederick retrieved his body for a burial in England. He eventually restructured and reorganized British troops to defeat Napoleon the First, the serpentine sponsored usurper. His attempts to rally the British were depicted in rhyme entitled the Grand Old Duke of York.

The sage of Monticello championed the false Declaration of Independence, legitimizing the struggle for freedom until the war was won. The British troops burned the homes of patriots on the Hudson River after the Sons of Liberty lured the captain into an ambush. They murdered him and his crew as the Lady Washington sailed away. The British soldiers did not support the traitors, even if the treachery favored them. The traitors had proved that they could not be trusted.

The traitors ran off with war funds secured by the pirates flying the flag of skull and bones. They stored their gold at Fort Knox for over a century. Some even became presidents, after a few assassinations. People unwittingly pledged allegiance to the subsidiary of the United India Company, dubbed the United States of America, divided by pirates, with liberty for whoever grabbed it, and justice for none.

Chapter Thirty

There is a lot to be said for inspiration

Sometimes that is all there is

Reference Tune: *Brave*

----Sara Bareilles

"THE EAGLES SOARED beyond the fraudulent Declaration of Independence, and this is their Eagle's Flight," Tobias later told Joan during a phone conservation. "The spirit of the Blue Heron survived. It grounded the inspiration imbued through the necklace given to Susan by her brothers. She used it as an aid to wade through the depths of consciousness."

"The story of the necklace transcends the initial yogic setting, which began in India. The Sons of Liberty, patriots, Tories, Loyalists, and fighters eventually all perished in the American Revolution---but who won?" Joan asked after he related the story. She added, "Nobody gets out of here alive, unless they are a vampire."

"Remember Prigogine's Theory of Dissipative Structures?" Tobias asked. "They gave him a Nobel Prize for describing the power of a seed, and the ability of coherent energies to regenerate the coded energy within the structure."

It varies according to the individual. What is incoherent dies. What is coherent thrives. The answer to your question pertains to the judgment of the living and the dead that Lincoln addressed in Gettysburg," Tobias replied. The immortality of the nation depended on grace, charm, and commitment."

"Those are attributes of coherent communication," Joan observed.

"That is why those involved claim that the music died in 1963," Tobias admitted. Everyone knew it, though the words were not heard. There was no song left to sing."

"It is not the money," Joan observed. "It is the symbolism, and what money means to some people."

"During the Civil War there were those who shamelessly fought on for the wrong reason, regardless of whether they were Confederate or Union," Tobias said, turning the conversation back to Gettysburg. "In the end, there is only light or dark. The dark never survives the light."

Joan added, "The dark side purposely contaminated the transport of souls between the dimensions. Lincoln broke the noose around the necks of the purely departed with his speech. "Liberty and justice for all is a double-edged sword, an unhealthy proposition. Not all deserve justice. Truth marches as swift as the fiery sword of the glory hallelujah of the Civil War song. Lincoln's friend Edgar Allan Poe gave us the 'gory' alleluia, the flip side to the glory."

"There's nothing like the words of a poet to document history. It beats raiders of lost arks."

"I agree. A poet's heart tells many tales."

"It is like the lyrics of songs, which honest people at the copyright office once considered shared information," Tobias mentioned. "More than ever, it has become important to listen to the backdrop of our lives, otherwise the songs and symbols become a subtle form of mind-control. Unlike words aligned with a musical rhythm or patter, prose tends to break up energy through the introduction of critical thinking. Songs can become lullabies, lulling a weakened state into sleep, whether it is healthy or not. People forget to exercise control, and reject what doesn't resonate or make sense."

"Separate the incoherent from the coherent."

"It is a mental function. Use it or lose it."

"The American Revolution erupted between the illusionists and realists," Joan summarized. "The use of the crystal required the skill of discrimination and critical thinking."

"It became alien warfare," Tobias shuddered. "Those in this country who demean the raptor symbolization are usually derivatives of the initial Transylvania exploitation, and out of harmony with nature. The natural world played a major role in the birth of the nation, even among those promoting the hoax of 1776."

"The nation died in 1775. A flame or seed survived with the help of the MidEarth."

"Despite the power plays, there was an innocence that pulled through," Tobias fathomed. "The necklace places the American Revolution in the context of high school, where the relationships are intense, yet fleeting. Nobody settles down because there is still more work to do. However, those stealing credit for the creation were guilty of spiritual abandonment."

Joan laughed. "People don't give credit to the cheerleaders; they give the win to the football team that played the game. This nation was seeded by a group of teenagers and the elders, who mentored them. It was a coed and multiracial movement."

Tobias leaned back in his chair by the phone. Looking at his notes, he added, "The captain of the Lexington militia died in the following battle in Concord. When faced with financial loss and care of her customers, Susan stood her ground like a heron. I suspect that she had TB as well as Parker. Her actions reflect the tuberculinic miasm."

"How's that?" Joan asked. She sighed before continuing, "Her spirit became energized and she fought for her rights. She reminds me of you, Tobias, and your romantic quest to make alternative medicine available to your clients."

"Yes, fortunately, I have balanced the internal tuberculinic terrain, so I am free to do my own thing without the hangups of the past," he quipped. Turning around in his chair, Tobias changed the subject slightly. "Lincoln wisely addressed the army at Gettysburg and remind them of the war's true significance."

Standing her ground on the comparisons between Tobias's situation and Susan's plight, Joan said, "I consider both of you as nurturing, evolved, and advanced spirits."

"Many lives have been lost from an unrealistic, unbalanced view of history," Tobias noted. He leaned over his desk with his elbows on the table. "A more appropriate term would be founding parents, but this is misleading. I think that we need a verb to denote action."

"Something short-lived to match the miasmatic terrain of tuberculosis," Joan suggested. "Little did the perpetrators know that they were seeding a nation on the blood of overstretched idealists, while they contaminated the colonies with TB. America needs a phrase that fits the romantic, far-reaching, impossible mission of the surviving guild of Black knights calling themselves Eagles."

"Oh, Susan proved grounded as a pragmatic, successful businesswoman. She never lived long enough to die from TB," Tobias said, ending the discussion. "She transcended the circumstances that threatened to entrap her, and her life became an Eagle's Flight."

BIBLIOGRAPHY

Andrews, Ted. Animal Speak. St. Paul, Minnesota. Llewellyn Publications. 1993.

Christy, Michael. Cooking Treasures of the Past. Charlottesville, Virginia. Historic Michie Tavern Museum. 1976.

Mount Vernon Ladies' Association of the Union. George Washington's Mount Vernon Official Guidebook. Mount Vernon, Virginia. 2001.

Staib, Walter. City Tavern Cookbook. Philadelphia: Running Press. 1999.

www.ingramcontent.com/pod-product-compliance
Lightning Source LLC
Chambersburg PA
CBHW050517190726
48284CB00003B/840